AN Earl LIKE ANY OTHER

THE GARDEN GIRLS

AN EARL LIKE ANY OTHER

BOOK TWO OF *THE GARDEN GIRLS* SERIES
JEMMA FROST

ALSO BY JEMMA FROST

Charming Dr. Forrester
All Rogues Lead to Ruin
An Earl Like Any Other
The Scoundrel Seeks a Wife

Copyright © 2022 The Arrowed Heart.
All rights reserved. No part of this publication may be reproduced, distributed, or transmitted in any form or by any means, including photocopying, recording, or other electronic or mechanical methods, without the prior written permission of the publisher, except in the case of brief quotations embodied in critical reviews and certain other noncommercial uses permitted by copyright law.

E-Book ISBN: 978-1-955138-06-2
Paperback ISBN: 978-1-955138-07-9

Any references to historical events, real people, or real places are used fictitiously. Names, characters, and places are products of the author's imagination.

Edited by Hazel Walshaw
Book Cover by The Arrowed Heart.
First printing edition 2022.

www.thearrowedheart.com

Dedicated to those of us still recovering from past trauma and discovering the layers of our emotions.

PROLOGUE

HAMPSHIRE, ENGLAND 1864

HE SHOULDN'T BE TOUCHING me.

Lily Taylor understood the rules of propriety. She knew the consequences of letting a man other than her husband take certain liberties with her body would not end well for her. Did she particularly care as the man in question's fingers massaged and tugged on her reddened nipples?

In a word? No.

Did that make her a harlot? A strumpet destined for a fiery afterlife? Perhaps. But then again, Lily found it difficult to muster much defense while her neighbor, Owen Lennox, kept his warm hands full of her breasts, and his mouth preoccupied her own.

"God, Lily, I adore how you feel," Owen murmured, pressing her forcefully into one of the stone columns surrounding them in their secret meeting spot—the lake gazebo.

"Mmm... I can tell." Her hips lifted to rock hard against his erection, wishing they had time for her to see it, touch it. But they were both expected home soon, so their illicit rendezvous needed to stay constrained to feverish kisses, though Owen had already broken the rule by ripping her dress open to reveal her pale chest to the sunlight.

What a sharp turn their relationship had taken.

Growing up together with his father's estate bordering her family home, the majority of their interactions had been arguments while her sisters observed from afar—varying degrees of amusement and exasperation on their faces. Spats Lily had relegated to standard back and forth between spirited friends.

But all those heated exchanges masked an attraction that had become undeniable over the past months. Since her eighteenth birthday, to be exact.

When a silly argument over the best flavor of cake ended with their lips finding each other in a haze of passion. Passion grown bolder as they acted upon their desires, as evidenced by today—the scrape of Owen's calloused palm imprinted on her chest where he'd slipped inside the loose linen to caress bare skin.

"Soon, we won't be stuck meeting like this. Won't be forced to restrain ourselves."

"To be fair, we don't restrict much," she admitted. They'd explored more of each other than they'd originally expected—at first trying to maintain decorum and proper courtship. Unfortunately, Owen and Lily both possessed fiery temperaments as evinced by past arguments; it seemed those same qualities applied to lust and desire, too, because their wills to be good hadn't been strong for long.

"True, but I want more. Need more." Owen nipped at her bottom lip. "I hate sneaking around so much. I want to parade you around on my arm during the day and have you at my bedside at night."

She yearned for those things, also, though she was a bit more pragmatic about their circumstances. He was Lord Ashland, first son of the Earl of Trent, and she was a country girl borne to a former professor. Their stations were not equal.

However, secluded in their small village and free to roam the countryside, it became too easy to forget such things as station and the line between them—a blurred line at this point. Though Lily didn't know many nobles, Owen didn't act superior to her or her family. They matched intellects consistently—his teachings from a private tutor, then university, while Papa taught her from home.

And despite her brashness, Owen never scolded or made her feel badly about some of the things she said or did that ordinary English girls wouldn't dare. He accepted her as she was—even loved her—and she recognized the gift such an act was. It mirrored her parents' marriage, unique interests and temperaments bound in the purest of loves.

"I feel the same way, but we mustn't rush. Your parents... They'll require time to become accustomed to the idea of us."

"They won't stop me. I'll make them see reason, and they'll love you as much as I do. It's not as if you don't already have their friendship."

Lily sighed, a sense of familiarity settling over her. They'd had this conversation before. It never ended satisfactorily, since neither of them pressed for a conclusion—an extraordinary outcome considering the way their usual tiffs concluded. "I know. I know." Seeing the waning sunlight turn orange and gold, she extracted herself from his hold, quickly doing up the buttons on her dress. "However, they may change their minds if they discovered I made you late for supper. We should head home."

Owen opened his mouth to argue but shut it after noting the beginning of sunset, too. Helping Lily right the rest of her dress and holding her hair ribbon as she rebraided the long strands, he placed another lingering kiss on her lips before walking her to the edge of the woods where they would part ways.

"I love you, Lily. Believe that. Believe in me."

Blushing at his fervent declaration, she smiled. "I love you, too. Now, go before we both get caught together." Shooing him away, she watched his disappearing form and then turned for her family's cottage, breaking into a run, too high in spirit for a mere walk home.

Lily's feet pounded against the dirt path, a brisk breeze ruffling the wisps of hair around her face, until she skidded to a halt outside the cottage and braced two hands on the white fence cordoning lush gardens from wild forest.

Mama would be happy to see her roses finally starting to bloom, she thought absentmindedly, as a glimpse of scarlet unfurled to her left. After their children, the Taylor couple's pride and joy lay with the flourishing foliage encapsulating their quaint home—especially now that Mr. Taylor had retired from teaching to focus on research.

Releasing a sigh of contentment, the chaotic energy coursing through her body slowly calmed as she stood still under the warm sun and closed her eyes to the brightness. She loved this place—the old cottage, the tangles of wildlife at her fingertips, and the lake and gazebo home to her and Owen's trysts.

Murmurs from inside floated on the air—girlish chatter—no doubt from Hazel describing another one of her stories to Iris and Caraway. As the youngest sister, she reaped the benefits of being the baby of the family, doted upon and indulged, while sharing the fantastical imaginings she created. Though Lily preferred living in the present reality, she admired her sister's ability to create and dream such detailed fictional tales.

Temperature cooled to a reasonable level after a few more minutes, she patted warm cheeks that she'd attribute to the weather and exercise if asked, rather than Owen's kisses, and stepped inside the cool interior of her home. Immediately, the familiar scents of baking and fresh flowers wound around her in the gentlest of bonds, and Lily breathed deeply, allowing it to draw her closer to her sisters huddled in the living area.

"Lily, you're back! And just in time." Hazel raced over with arms full of old clothing. At sixteen, a youthful exuberance clung to her awkward limbs. "We were about to rehearse the scene between Alessia and Aqua the Mermaid."

What fun...

"Must we do this now?" *Or at all, considering they weren't little girls anymore.* But she kept that thought to herself.

All Lily really wanted to do was take a nap and relive the afternoon with Owen.

"If we have to participate, so do you." Caraway, the eldest sister, sat in a worn armchair reading over a sheet of paper in her hands.

"It'll be fun. Don't be a sourpuss," Iris said from her perch by the fireplace. Technically a cousin, she'd been raised as a Taylor sister after her mother—Lily's aunt—abandoned her as a baby. "Oh, how was your ramble through the woods today?"

Renewed heat brought a blush to her cheeks. "Agreeable. You know there's nothing ever exciting to report. The path around the lake remains the same."

"We thought you might have seen Owen. That's what she's trying to get at," Caraway explained, a no-nonsense gleam in her eyes.

"I think you mean Lord Ashland," Hazel corrected.

"He may be a lord, but he's also very nearly a brother to us. Even if he hadn't told us on numerous occasions to call him by his given name, I would. We're too familiar."

The one break in Caraway's usually propriety-conscious mind.

Trying to keep her tone neutral—empty of her true feelings—Lily asked, "Why would you think Owen and I would've met?" Her sisters weren't oblivious; it wouldn't surprise her if they suspected something between her and their neighbor's son. But Lily couldn't fathom how they'd learn about the intimate meetings at the lake gazebo.

How could they, unless one of them managed to follow behind her daily romps traversing uneven ground and fallen boughs? And the only one capable of such a feat was Hazel with her nimble feet.

"Mrs. Holly stopped for a visit while you were gone. She relayed the message of his return from Cambridge. We wondered if he'd be walking the lake while you were out."

The tension in her shoulders loosened as she bent to wiggle a makeshift mermaid's tail onto her stockinged feet. A reasonable assumption based on Mrs. Holly's information, not because Lily's emotions were displayed for all and sundry to see.

She'd learned of Owen's arrival yesterday when she'd found a note from him tucked into their hiding spot, setting up their meeting today. Their secret form of communication had been her idea after a particularly long spat of time without seeing each other. They'd needed a way to connect when popping into the other's home randomly was out of the question.

"Oh, he must be spending time with Lord and Lady Trent." A troubled huff escaped as she yanked the too-small tail up her calves.

"You're probably right. Now that he's nearing his majority, I'm sure preparations are being made for a betrothal." Hazel plopped onto the rug-covered floor and flipped through her own lines for the play.

The nonchalant declaration caused Lily's hand to jolt, and a ripping sound filled the room.

"Lily, you tore the seam!"

Glancing down, ragged threads and her cream stocking peeked through where the patched scales of a mermaid tail should have been. "I'm sorry. It was an accident."

Caraway sighed, then waved a hand in dismissal. "No matter. We'll fix it later."

Nodding, Lily asked the question foremost in her mind. "To my knowledge, there hasn't been talk of a courtship. Why would there be a betrothal? Did Mrs. Holly mention something?"

"No, but eventually he'll need a countess. Might as well start the search early," Iris answered with a shrug of her thin shoulders. An ethereal creature come to life, she more resembled a fairy or nymph than a flesh and blood girl of nineteen.

Caraway continued, "You know how these things work with the nobility. Frankly, I'm surprised he hasn't been promised to someone since birth."

Iris and Hazel agreed, their muted voices fading to the background as Lily's mind flashed to a previous conversation—one of promises made and societal rules broken. Discussion of marriage despite differing stations.

And she regretted ever giving into such fantasies.

What was I thinking? This isn't one of Hazel's stories.

Living in Shoreham, a quaint village in Hampshire, it was easy to ignore society's expectations. As part of the eccentric Taylor family, she was used to feeling separate.

But those things didn't apply to Owen, an earl's son—no matter how far away they lived from society's epicenter. Especially since his family already possessed a mark against them with the current earl's marriage to the daughter of a wealthy Irish businessman, the Trent title needing an influx of funds more than a proper societal match.

"I hope she's not too snobbish, whoever she is," Hazel said, interrupting Lily's spiral into despair. "It'd be a shame if we couldn't see Owen anymore."

Snobbish or not, Lily would avoid the couple—it'd be too painful seeing him with another woman. A beautiful noblewoman who wouldn't bring unwanted judgment to his family name. A lady born and bred for an esteemed position as a countess, not a country girl who'd never dreamed of holding such a place in Owen's life until recently.

It'll be worse if we continue down this path.

She needed to put an end to their liaisons.

Owen would refuse to listen to reason, she knew. He could be as stubborn as an ox when he wanted to be, which was anytime they were together, when he wanted to spark a playful row. He'd brush aside her concerns over his family's legacy, over her lack of education when it came to society expectations.

So, it had to be her.

But how?

A simple breaking of their relationship wouldn't be possible. Forget the past few months of kisses and touches. They had years of friendship behind them. Owen would fight her, even if she was doing it to save both of them from future heartbreak.

"That day is far off, I'm sure. Are we going to rehearse? If not, I can get back to the handkerchief I'm embroidering for Mama's birthday." Iris tensed as if to leave until Hazel put a staying hand on her knee.

"No, no, we'll start now." She cleared her throat. "We open on a ship..."

Lily listened with half an ear as the future she'd dared to dream about with Owen dissolved in the face of reality. A lone tear tracked down her cheek, which she swiftly brushed away before her sisters could notice.

Stop being dramatic.

Common sense fought for supremacy. They were young, not truly in love.

Yet, it didn't soothe her as she'd hoped.

A passing childhood fancy or not, Owen—Lord Ashland—and she could never be together.

And it was up to her to break both of their hearts before true, permanent damage occurred.

TWO DAYS LATER

HIS FRIENDS LAUGHED when he bragged about marrying the girl of his dreams. They thought him imbecilic for tying himself to one woman at so young an age. Men were supposed to sow wild oats, traverse the world, and indulge in its delights—namely, women.

But Owen had never yearned for that sort of life. His parents loved each other despite a business contract preceding their marriage, and he held high hopes for his own love match.

And fortunately, the woman in question lived right next door.

Lily Taylor.

He adored her, plain and simple. She drove him mad with longing, from her teasing smile to their fiery arguments, and even more recently, with her kisses.

Yes, Lily Taylor would be his wife and the next Countess of Trent.

They would spend their lives together in Hampshire near both of their families, and eventually children would be raised in the same grassy knolls they'd played in, swim the same lake. Honestly, he couldn't wait.

AN EARL LIKE ANY OTHER 11

Heading towards the stables for his daily ride, Owen entered with a sense that all was right in his world.

Until the vision before him sent it crashing to the ground in a blazing inferno.

Lily—*his Lily*—stood in the arms of one of the stableboys, Asa Lynch. Her lips touched Lynch's in a facsimile of what they'd shared only the day before, and a peculiar cracking originated in his chest. "Lily?" Surely that odd croak hadn't come from him, yet it must have because two pairs of eyes turned to stare at him—one set arrogant and the other pained, or so he thought before it disappeared beneath a cloud of determination.

"My lord, I wasn't expecting you." Lynch had the gall to lie.

"I come for my horse, Hercules, every day at two. Can't imagine how it slipped your mind, though I can see you've got your hands quite full at the moment." Lily scrambled to fasten three undone buttons at the top of her dress, and he noticed strands of hair trailing from her braid as if Lynch had dug *his* hands into the coiffure, holding her close for *his* touch.

Owen couldn't look at her any longer. Didn't want to say her name, let alone think it.

How could she betray him this way?

Why would she do this to them?

They'd talked of love, of marriage. They'd made promises to each other.

He was going to tell his father about his decision, convince him of its rightness, despite the lack of her station as the daughter of a former professor. Earls were powerful in their own right, as were their sons. If he chose to marry below his class according to society, then he would and be happy to rub their noses in it.

Except Lily kissed Lynch. In Owen's stables.

And did more by the looks of her disheveled dress and hair.

She'd broken his heart in one fell swoop, and suddenly, the gentle caution his father offered, the laughter of his friends, caught up to him. He'd been a fool to believe in such things as happy endings. To trust the affections of an eighteen-year-old girl. A girl who'd always bucked tradition, down to the very breeches she wore now after clearly coming here after a walk about the forest.

"Leave. Now." He motioned for the open door behind him. Lily scurried past. Her steps faltered as she drew even with his shoulders but continued forward without a word. What could she say, anyway? Apologies would be useless. Especially now, with the blood running high in his veins.

"I said I needed Hercules. Is it not your job to do my bidding?" The most imperious tone he could muster blurted out, and Lynch snapped to attention—saddling Owen's horse before sauntering away, unable to resist another smirk.

The bastard.

Mounting his chestnut horse, Owen cantered forward until they reached a private stretch of land, and he gave Hercules freedom to run. The blistering wind chapped his cheeks as they flew across the Hampshire countryside. Recklessness chased their tail, and Owen almost wished there were obstacles to jump—to conquer—because he itched to release the pain sloshing around in his gut.

"Goddammit!" The epithet shouted into the air, carried away to oblivion, encapsulating the raging emotions threatening to drown him under their weight. Conflicting emotions spanning the spectrum of love and hate.

And he loathed the weak part of him that didn't immediately kill every last ounce of love he harbored for Lily. *Give it time, and she'll fade to a painful memory.* Yes, time. And space. That's what he needed.

Owen recalled one of his compatriots embarking on a tour of the Continent soon. Miles Brandon, while frustrating at times, certainly knew how to enjoy life. Something his suddenly tattered life needed desperately.

Slowing Hercules to a calmer pace, they turned back home as Owen plotted for an extended stay abroad because the more he pondered the idea, the more enticing it became. His parents wouldn't begrudge him a jaunt around the world, and the intrigues of new locales would distract Owen from the impetus of his trip.

I'll leave for a few months, maybe even a year, and when I return, a certain neighboring woman will be a footnote in my past.

Lily Taylor—love of his life, betrayer of his love—would no longer matter to him.

CHAPTER ONE

HAMPSHIRE, ENGLAND 1871

SEVEN YEARS LATER

EARLY MORNING LIGHT lit the stranger from behind, casting a long shadow across the wood floor—a shadow that stopped inches from where Lily remained seated, studying the newcomer. The dark shading and its owner's unceremonious arrival before proper visiting hours did not bode well in her mind as the buttered toast she'd swallowed turned to a sick pit in her stomach.

Who was this man?

An unfamiliar presence who dared to intrude on their morning breakfast without an invitation.

"Good morning." He executed a brief bow, a wiry lock of hair falling forward. The hat in his hand tapped against his thigh as he waited to be let in.

Caraway, Lily's eldest sister, had answered the summons at the door, and she dipped her head in greeting. "Good morning, sir. May I help you?"

"You're one of Mr. Phinneas Taylor's daughters, I presume?"

"Yes, I'm the eldest Miss Caraway Taylor, then my sisters, Miss Iris and Miss Lily." Cara gestured to them as they both stood, dipping their chins in greeting, curiosity and wariness shimmering from them. It was unusual for them to receive guests as they didn't possess many friends in the nearby village, and a male visitor was even rarer.

"How do you do, ladies? My name is Mr. Edward Laramie. I've recently returned from an extended trip to South America and have urgent business to conduct with your father if he's available."

The women cast identical looks of shock at the man before Cara ushered him inside. "Please take a seat, Mr. Laramie. Would you care for some refreshment? Tea?"

He shook his head and set his hat on the kitchen table the four of them sat around. As if sensing the indoor tension, the atmosphere remained quiet—no cheerful chirping floating in through the windows or scratching of squirrels as they climbed the nearby oak.

It unsettled Lily.

A sensation that intensified when Laramie's gaze traveled over each woman before landing on her and narrowing. Uncomfortable at the perusal of his inhumanly light eyes, she swiftly attempted to throw him off with a challenging stare of her own. To no avail.

Old breeches formed to her crossed legs while the oversized cotton shirt she wore billowed around her. She usually ate breakfast in such attire, since they made her brisk morning strolls easier. However, the thin clothing felt non-existent at Laramie's persistent study.

Clearing her throat, oblivious to the interaction, Cara patted the buttons on her dress in a nervous gesture before dropping a hand to her lap. "I'm afraid speaking with our father won't be possible. Our parents died in a carriage accident almost two years ago. I'm sorry you haven't heard the news yet."

A grunt of surprise left Mr. Laramie as his eyes finally left Lily to focus on a leather case where he retrieved a sheaf of papers. An odd mark below his ear caught her attention, a brownish-black mole or freckle of some kind. "That is unfortunate... My condolences." His eyes met Lily's again, and she forced her gaze upward again, to not look away. "However, it doesn't negate a serious breach of contract on your father's part."

The abrupt change of tone—from apologetic to business-like—grated, but Lily withheld a sharp retort.

It wouldn't do to insult the man... yet.

He tossed what she assumed to be the contract on the table between the plate of toast slices and a pitcher of cream. The resounding thump caused waves in the milky liquid, a tsunami of problems hurtling down to drown them under its weight.

Lily snatched the bundle of parchment from its ominous position and skimmed over the bold lines of script. "It appears that Mr. Laramie commissioned a research project from Papa where he combined Mr. Laramie's research and his own into one comprehensive book on bryophytes." Raising an eyebrow in silent question, her sisters shook their heads simultaneously. No one knew what a bryophyte was.

"It was supposed to be *the* book on bryophytes, part of my legacy as a scholarly explorer. As I said earlier, for the past year and a half, I've been exploring remote parts of South America working on my next project. Correspondence was nonexistent, but I expected your father to have the finished product when I arrived." The man rested clasped hands on the table as he leaned forward. "Do you know if he was able to complete the project before his demise?"

"I hardly think so. The date on this contract says it was signed September 1869; our father passed in October," Lily explained and handed the contract to Caraway to read for herself. A large advance had been paid to Papa, and while they hadn't been frivolous with expenses, their family certainly didn't have the full amount to repay Mr. Laramie.

Lily wondered how benevolent he'd turn out to be, how far his condolences would extend. To forgive the debt in its entirety? Allow for a repayment plan?

An inward shudder ran through her. No, she doubted they'd be so fortunate.

We never are...

"It seems we're in a bit of a quandary then, girls," he said condescendingly, and an angry flush welled on Lily's cheeks. "Seeing as I've no book, it's only fair that I receive recompense for the sum I paid your father before my departure."

"But, we don't have—" Iris started, but Cara cut her off with a hand on her arm and a quick shake of her head.

"Naturally. However, as three single women still grieving our parents, I beseech your sense of compassion and generosity. A sum such as this is unattainable at the moment, but we're willing to repay you in installments if that's agreeable." A shrewd look entered Cara's blue eyes, and for once, Lily was thankful for her sister's take-charge attitude.

Usually, it rubbed her the wrong way—she didn't like being told what to do. But in this case, it was a relief to let her older sister handle the issue.

"My sympathies for your situation, but I'm afraid that won't be possible. I won't reap the benefits of my research from this last trip until months from now. This book was meant to cover the intervening lull." Collecting his hat and bag, Mr. Laramie shifted to his feet and motioned to the contract. "That is a duplicate for your own records."

"But, sir, please—"

"I'm not an unfeeling man, Misses Taylor. Therefore, I'll give you a fortnight to gather the necessary funds. If you can't manage the task, I'll be forced to contact my barrister and sue for breach of contract. It might result in the loss of this lovely cottage, as it's sold to cover the cost." Mr. Laramie bowed, once again, his eyes finding Lily's.

If only that unbecoming mark was on his nose, she thought uncharitably, frustrated by the morning's turn of events.

"Farewell, ladies. I wish you luck." And he saw himself out, the quiet shutting of the door resembling a death knell as they remained paralyzed in their seats.

"I can't believe this."

"What are we going to do?" Iris ran a hand over her chignon before her head fell to her hands in anguish.

Sudden energy flooded her veins after the bombshell. Lily hopped to her feet, an irrepressible need to escape building in her bones.

"There's nothing for it. Looks like we're going to be homeless in a fortnight, so we better start packing what we want to keep before it's auctioned off."

Repeatedly, fate reminded the Taylor family that nothing would ever go their way. Lily didn't understand how her sisters thought this would be any different.

First, their parents died. Then Hazel left. And now this.

Don't forget Owen. You couldn't have him either.

Lily sneered at the bothersome inclusion, a weak spot in her mind to be sure, and reminded herself that she didn't care anymore.

I don't want him.

"Lily Nicole, don't say such things! How can you be so cruel?" Cara reprimanded with a firm swat on the wooden tabletop to punctuate her point.

"It's not cruel if it's the truth, and unless you've hoarded some secret treasure like the heroines in Hazel's fairytales, then a fortnight from now, we will be forced out of our home. Of all people, you should recognize the practicality of accepting that fact now rather than later." Stretching an arm over her head and pulling it down with the other before switching sides, she dared Cara to argue with a glare. "Now, if you'll excuse me, I'm going out for some much-needed air and exercise. Might be one of the last times I get to see the lake."

"You can't abandon us now. We need to…"

But the rest of Iris's words were cut off as Lily slammed the door behind her and took off in a sprint towards the woods and her favorite spot in all of Hampshire: the stone gazebo by the lake.

CHAPTER TWO

Owen Lennox, the ninth Earl of Trent, heard rapid footfalls and rustling brush before Miss Lily Taylor emerged from the line of oak trees.

They hadn't spoken in months, not since their accidental run-in last winter while she ambled around the lake with her sister Hazel. She'd been frostier than the December chill, avoiding his gaze and promptly excusing herself from his presence. He'd willed her to acknowledge him, yet she'd remained steadfast in evading any sort of conversation.

Since then, they'd managed to dodge being thrown together again. A feat, considering the lake and gazebo were their favorite places to hide when seeking peace.

Which is why he'd come this morning. Home for seven months, and it was starting to weigh on him.

Best get used to it. This is the rest of your life.

Sighing at the inevitability of his future, Owen rested against a marble column as his gray eyes tracked Lily's progress—studied the woman who was supposed to feature prominently in said future.

Until she betrayed me.

Owen had promised her forever, then he caught her with a stablehand in the barn.

News had traveled like wildfire after Asa Lynch told his friends what the Taylor girl let him do. Fists clenched, Owen tried to regulate his breathing as he recalled that Sunday when the gossip-mongering had reached a fever pitch, yet he'd been expected to pretend it didn't matter to him.

An earl's son couldn't marry a former professor's daughter.

Except I would have found a way if not for her duplicitous actions.

Lily skipped over the four stones set in the small lake offshoot. Water streamed from the lake to surround the old gazebo, creating a secret island that he'd always loved. With spring blooming into summer, willow trees surrounded the island, adding to the intimate setting.

When she finally noticed him, he thought he saw the briefest glimpse of pleasure before it disappeared under a crush of annoyance. "What are you doing here?" Her sharp tone sliced through the serene atmosphere. But she didn't run from him. Instead, Lily hopped the last stone to the gazebo steps and marched inside.

"Last I checked, this land belongs to me. It's due to my generosity that you've been allowed to freely dash about." *Opening salvo to me*, he thought, as the familiar cadence of their arguments settled over him.

A bark of laughter tinged with bitterness burst from Lily. "Ah, yes, I must be careful. Any more so-called generosity from men, and I'm liable to keel over." She tore a leaf from one of the climbing vines wrapped around a column, the vicious act putting him on guard.

His Lily was in a mood today.

Not yours.

"What's that supposed to mean?" He straightened to his full height to frown down at her statuesque form. As one of the taller women in Shoreham, Owen appreciated not having to crane his neck to speak with her. *Or kiss her.*

His gaze dropped to the plump bottom lip he'd obsessed over ever since he'd reached an age to notice such things about the opposite sex. It'd been years since their last kiss, and he shouldn't be interested in repeating the act after what she'd done. But her draw remained like a bloody oasis in the desert, beckoning him for the slightest drink.

Pathetic.

"Only that I'm sick of men purporting to be gentlemen, revealing their true underhanded colors in a guise of generosity and kindness," she huffed, pacing in a half-moon, never crossing to his side of the gazebo. "I don't care if you own this land. I wouldn't care if you owned all of bloody Hampshire! I'll go where I want when I want, and there's nothing you or any other man can do about it."

"Speaking of guises, I see you've dropped any pretense of being a lady—swearing like a common sailor."

Wearing breeches that showcased her legs.

Letting another man touch her when she belonged to me.

"I never pretended to be a lady. If you've been operating under that misconception all these years, then I pity your future progeny, for they're sure to be slow indeed." The insult shouldn't amuse him—shouldn't arouse him—but this was the first time Lily had chosen to spend more than a minute in his presence and engage in any kind of dialogue. It almost felt like old times with their fiery bickering.

Something you should forget or else prove her assessment of your intelligence correct.

"How fortunate you no longer need worry about my future children." The pointed barb met its mark as she flinched, and he resisted offering an immediate apology—the least she could do was feel guilty for what she'd done.

A strong wind blew through the gazebo, bringing the sweet smell of lily—her namesake. But it would take more than the serene tableau surrounding them to defuse this situation.

Once they began, they always saw things through to the end because neither of them could resist a victory over the other.

Marching forward, Lily stopped short from giving him the slap he was sure itched at her palm. Instead, she opted to keep her hands loose at her sides, as if preparing for a future wallop along his head, and fixed turbulent eyes on him. Hazel eyes turned golden in anger—one of the reasons he used to antagonize her, to view the extraordinary change.

"As if I ever needed to concern myself with such a topic as your heirs." Her gaze dropped momentarily to his lips before glancing to the side then back at him. She knew it was a lie, yet held her ground.

Her blatant denial of their past relationship scraped along his insides and tempted him to remind her exactly how intimate they'd been. Especially when Lily angled away as if to dismiss him.

Don't be a fool.

Ignoring the warning, he grasped her hips roughly, yanking her body into his—soft molding to firm—and stopped her retreat. Forcing a rebuttal through gritted teeth, he taunted,

"Is that so? If memory serves, we were one tryst away from my taking your virtue until you gave it away to Lynch. Shall I help you recall that final afternoon?"

Her nails dug into his shoulders where he expected to be pushed away, but the push didn't come. Intent on raising her ire higher, he continued, "What's one more, after all? You've already given yourself away, haven't you?" The harsh words burned as he spoke them, but he couldn't resist trying to make her feel the pain raging inside him.

"That's what you think of me, isn't it?"

"Why shouldn't I? Do you deny it?" How he wished she would, but Lily remained quiet.

Damn her.

And damn him.

Taking advantage of the hesitation, Owen crushed his mouth to hers in a punishing kiss, his meager resistance crumbling under the rush of old habits. Each fought for supremacy as their tongues dueled—refusing to let the other one win the upper hand.

He'd missed this.

A fair share of women had thrown themselves at the Englishman with a title and money to spare as he traveled throughout the Continent these past years. And on occasion, Owen would even entertain their feminine wiles, giving into clandestine meetings and scandalous kisses, but he never let it go past a certain point.

Because of Lily.

No matter how much she hurt him. How little he trusted her. How impossible it would be for anything to grow between them again.

Despite numerous valid reasons, Owen couldn't bring himself to touch another woman the way he'd once touched her, once dreamed of loving her.

So, here he stood, a damned virgin nearing thirty, kissing the woman he loved at twenty as if the years and betrayal in between meant nothing.

You are a damned, bloody fool.

OWEN'S LARGE HANDS flexed on her hips, and Lily knew she'd have marks later from the bruising hold. Perfect to commemorate her stupidity.

She allowed herself one more minute of his possession, to relax in the freedom of familiarity and ignore all the alarms sounding in her head. The time to dwell on those and curse her weakness would come soon enough, after all.

Spicy cinnamon forced a moan of delight from her. Clearly, Owen still enjoyed those special candies from the confectioners' shop—a flavor she'd studiously avoided since their separation. As she'd avoided most things that brought memories of Owen to the forefront.

It hurt that he'd so easily believed Asa's word that Sunday.

While Lily had planned for Owen to catch her in a compromising position, she hadn't foreseen Asa spreading rumors fabricating further intimacies to the whole village. The fact that Owen thought she could commit such acts reinforced the knowledge that she'd made the right decision to end their relationship.

He was supposed to be upset, angry that she'd been unfaithful to a certain extent—not by providing sexual favors to another man.

You got what you wanted. You set out to ruin the relationship. Mussed hair, unbuttoned dress, and all. Don't quibble now because it went too far.

But I didn't want him to hate me.

The broken expression he wore after catching her and Asa still haunted her nightmares. Sometimes she even imagined what she should've said that day instead of leaving silently.

Nothing spoken would've erased his pain.

A well of sorrow rose in her gut—overwhelming in its intensity despite seven years passing—and Lily shoved at Owen, tearing her lips from his.

"You've made your point," she said raggedly before making her escape, leaping from stone to stone until reaching solid ground and racing into cover under the massive trees bordering the lake.

"Lily!" Owen called out her name, but she didn't look back.

She'd done enough of that in the past half hour to last a lifetime.

Diverging from the worn path, Lily ducked under low-hanging branches and jumped over fallen boughs when her foot came down on wet leaves, and she slammed to the ground with a grunt. Lying in the muck of damp earth, the wind knocked out of her lungs, Lily closed her eyes and tried to inhale calm breaths.

So rarely these days did she find any sort of peace—a break from the unrelenting pressure swirling inside. The explosive kiss with Owen had provided a measure of release. Allocated her family's trouble with Mr. Laramie to the background, and even deeper, eclipsed the dark turmoil blotting her soul, a constant companion ever since that fateful day years ago.

Relaxing under the loamy smell of the forest floor, Lily let her mind drift until the sun moved to beat overhead, signaling the afternoon. If only she could lay here forever.

Here lies Lily Nicole Taylor. Scandalous traitor of Owen Lennox and vexatious sister to Caraway, Iris, and Hazel.

Her headstone would disappear under mossy overgrowth, and no one would ever bother her again. *Nor she, them.*

Are you done wallowing yet?

Right, time to return to reality—bleak reality.

Shallow imprints pressed into the dirt as she dragged herself to her feet, mentally preparing to walk home. Upon her entry to the cottage, she heard someone rummaging in the study and found Caraway rifling through scattered sheets of paper that consumed every piece of flat space to be found.

"What is all of this?" she asked, and saw Iris shrug in resignation.

"Cara believes we can try to compile the research into a book ourselves."

"That's ridiculous! We don't know anything about bryophytes or how to go about doing Papa's part of the research."

Iris lifted the book in her hands. "Bryophytes are species of moss, so there's one thing we know."

"We've spent years watching our parents work. We're smart, capable women. It's worth a try unless you have a better idea," Cara snipped from her place at Papa's desk. The room remained mostly the same despite his absence, as they only ventured inside to dust every week. Otherwise, his books lay open with a pair of spectacles resting on one, as if he'd stepped out for a brief recess before returning to his work.

If only that were true.

Multiple frames showcased Mama's sketches and paintings of plants in various stages of growth, a testament to her own botanical interests. What a pair their parents had made.

Iris interjected quietly. "I suggested writing to Hazel and Jonathan. Perhaps they can help in some way."

"They're in their first year of marriage and busy opening the boarding house along with Hazel's classes. They don't have the time or funds to help us. It would cause unnecessary worry." Leave it to Cara to shoulder the responsibility, protecting Hazel as she'd tried to protect all of them at one point or another. Flipping another sheet of parchment over, she continued her search through the disorganized mess.

What she thought to find Lily couldn't fathom.

Their father was notorious for being a bit scatter-brained and followed his own sorting system. Not to mention barely having time to work on Mr. Laramie's project before the accident that took him and Mama and almost Hazel. She doubted much of anything useful would be discovered.

"Maybe we should follow Hazel's lead and resign ourselves to leaving Hampshire. Maybe it'll be the blessing we need like it was for her." Skepticism coated the sentiment, but she supposed it could prove true for Cara and Iris.

"We're not leaving, and I wish you'd stop stating it as if it's fact."

Her agitated growl caused Cara to shoot a scowl in response before her gaze took a deliberate pass over Lily's disheveled clothing. "Why are you covered in mud and grass? You've got a streak of it across your cheek here, too." She motioned to her left cheek, and Lily untucked her shirt to use part of the clean hem to wipe it away.

"I tripped over an exposed tree root." No need to mention who'd occupied her mind so surely to distract her from such dangers.

"Are you okay?" Iris asked in concern.

Waving a dismissive hand, she nodded, leaning against the door frame to observe the chaos before her. "Nothing that hasn't happened before or won't happen again. I'm fine."

"Good. We wouldn't want you injured before the dowager countess's birthday ball."

Damnation. She'd forgotten about the ball for Owen's mother. "We're attending? Won't we be out of place as the country bumpkins?"

"You may refer to yourself as a bumpkin, but I take umbrage at the term." Cara sniffed, her pert nose wrinkled in disgust. "And of course, we're going. Her ladyship has been nothing but kind and invited us personally when I saw her at Millie's the other day."

"But what will we wear?"

"The gowns leftover from my short jaunt in London."

"Those old things!" Iris voiced the exact worry coursing through Lily.

Made for Cara's time in London after she turned eighteen, when she'd been hoping to find a husband while their father taught, they were going on a decade old. Moths should have eaten straight through them at this point.

"They're the only suitable garments we have for a party at the home of nobility unless you'd prefer to stick out like a sore thumb in our Sunday best." Cara gestured to the current cotton dress she wore whose blue trim differentiated it from the Sunday gown with gray. "We'll tailor them to fit both of you, though yours will be tough Lily with the height difference. And while we're making the adjustments, we'll bring them into this year's fashion trends."

Either way, we're going to look terrible.

Lily groaned and covered her eyes in shame. It was bad enough she'd have to see Owen after their recent interlude, but to have him see her dressed in home-stitched hand-me-downs while surrounded by beautiful women in silk and lace would be unbearable.

Perhaps I can claim a migraine...

Something she dealt with regularly these days, so it wouldn't be too far out of the realm of possibility.

"With your attitude, the gown won't be the problem. Try being optimistic for once."

Lily ignored the insult, too focused on creating a plan to escape attending the ball. Once, she'd been what Cara wanted—optimistic, blind to life's bitterness. But the truth had been revealed to her, and there was no going back to that young, naive girl.

"Good luck with your futile search." She swept an arm out to encompass the massive, cluttered desk. "I'm going to wash up. Maybe by then you'll have come to your senses."

Cara crumpled a scrap of paper and threw it at Lily in exasperation. "Doubtful. Now, get on with you! How I got saddled with sisters so..."

Lily laughed as she missed the end of her sibling's diatribe. At least some things would never change, even if their home did. The sobering thought quieted her as she filled a bowl with water in the kitchen before going upstairs for privacy.

Home. What did it really mean, anyway?

The cottage hadn't felt much like home after the death of their parents. All it really represented was a moratorium to their memory, no matter how hard they tried to carry on without them.

A change of scenery may not be a tragedy, after all.

CHAPTER THREE

A week after the incident with Lily, Owen strolled into his mother's morning room to find her sitting with Miles Brandon, the third son of Lord Bartley—a close friend of his late father's which meant Brandon and he had known each other since they were children.

Forced proximity created a tenuous friendship between the two sons—a friendship that grew more dubious as they grew older. At times, Owen appreciated Brandon's bombastic personality and need for constant entertainment, since it echoed his old spontaneous nature before Lily's betrayal and his father's death. But mostly, his wild ways incensed Owen, who wished the man would mature enough to reflect his age.

"There you are," his mother exclaimed with a note of relief that amused him. It seemed as if he wasn't the only one who needed to take their family friend in small doses these days. "Dear Brandon was telling me about one of your jaunts in Italy."

"I've arrived just in time to save you the sordid tale, then." He shot a cease and desist glare towards Brandon, who lounged indolently on the settee, legs spread wide as he sipped his cup of tea. The periwinkle blue of his frock coat matched the wallpaper coverings, and Owen wondered if he'd intended the coordination.

"Leave it to you to end our fun," the man groused.

"Not entirely. I've come to discuss the ball. Are you prepared to be bombarded by guests, Mama?"

The dowager smoothed a hand over the striped silk of her day gown and smiled. "I look forward to the gifts and a chance for my son to inspect prospective brides."

A coughing fit erupted from Brandon at the implication, but Owen ignored him. He knew this conversation would come up sooner or later—the fact that she'd waited seven months as he settled in after his travels proved a boon. But the ball would be the first societal function they'd host since his return, so he supposed it was natural she'd use it as an excuse to broach the topic.

At least it shan't be as overwhelming as it would be if we had it in London for the Season.

Thank goodness his mother had opted to stay with him in the country.

"The night's meant to celebrate you—not serve as a marriage mart." He took a seat opposite her. "I'm not interested in marrying any time soon, so I'd advise against raised hopes."

Marrying at all lacked interest from him these days, but as an earl, it was his duty to continue the line. He figured years from now he'd tie himself to some poor young chit, but that was a long way off. And certainly not while Lily remained so near.

"I don't see why we can't kill two birds with one stone," she explained, a calculated gleam in her eyes. "And it would be the greatest birthday gift a mother could ask for—her son happily married with future grandchildren soon to come."

The happy part's debatable.

"Yes, have a care for your mother's wishes, Trent," Brandon teased from his seat, well aware that he faced no danger of the parson's noose as a third son. While his family would like to see him settled, it wasn't necessary for him to produce an heir.

"Stay out of this." Owen pointed at Brandon in exasperation before turning to his mother. "And you...content yourself with me for the foreseeable future. If you're in dire need of interaction with little ones, I'm sure we can find one of the village children to keep you company."

"You can't remain a bachelor forever." Sunlight glinted off her auburn hair—the same rich color as his own—as she shook her head in denial, stubborn lines deepening the frown on her face.

"I'm not saying forever. I'm saying not now or in the near future." A battle of wills warred between them until she relented with a sigh, and like a pardoned prisoner having the rope removed from his neck, relief at the reprieve loosened the stiffness tightening his muscles—the war not won, but a small victory at least.

"I only wish for your happiness. I don't like how isolated you've been since you've returned home," she said, her expression softening. "A good wife would ease some of your burdens."

Not when the woman he wanted fought him at every turn.

You don't want her; you want who you thought she was.

"My lady, with respect, Trent's like any young buck. When he's finished sowing his wild oats, I'm sure he'll settle into respectable domesticity. Until then..." Brandon lifted his hands in resignation while Owen took offense at the reference of his oats in front of his mother, but the man never cared for propriety.

They'd cut a swath across the Continent together—Brandon landing them in trouble and Owen getting them out. If he hadn't been living in a numbed state for the past seven years, fraught with regrets and pain, he might have abandoned their wild trek, but the shameful truth was he'd needed the escape into Brandon's reckless adventures.

"Is that true? Because I confess to disbelief. You don't act like a man enjoying his bachelorhood." His mother made a fair point, knowing him all too well. Most days consisted of meeting with tenants, seeing to their needs, or dealing with the multiple ledgers outlining investments and other financial accounts—hardly relaxing matters.

However, he derived a certain satisfaction from upholding his duties to the people under his care, even if most men of his stature preferred leaving the majority of such work to land managers. But his father had seen to the workings of the estate personally, and Owen intended to continue the tradition and emulate the man he sought to live up to.

"I enjoy it well enough," he replied. "Now, can we return to the original subject? Is everything set for tomorrow night? Any last-minute changes I need to be aware of?"

"They're not changes, but you should know I invited the Taylor girls." The comment sounded innocuous enough, except for the slight dare in her voice. "I ran into Miss Taylor in the village and didn't think it would be right to celebrate without our closest neighbors, especially with the lot of you growing up so closely together."

"Miss Taylor...she's the eldest of four sisters, correct?" Brandon asked as he leaned forward to brace thin arms on his knees.

Owen regarded the man with irritation. "Can't you remember? You've met her about a dozen times during your visits during our school holidays."

"That was years ago. I can't be expected to recall every woman I've ever met." It would be nearly impossible with the way he ran through them anyway—the key point Brandon left out.

"She accepted the invitation?"

"Naturally. It would be rude to deny an invitation from the person of honor." And Caraway followed polite etiquette. She'd never risk rudeness if she could help it. Which meant Lily would be in attendance.

His mother carried on as if nothing was amiss. "That bad business involving Miss Lily is water under the bridge, as far as I'm concerned. To be honest, I never fully trusted that boy's iteration of events."

This was the first he'd heard her opinion on the matter. He'd never discussed his plans for Lily with his parents—didn't know for certain how they'd respond despite their unconventional ways. Though, he always assumed his mother would offer immediate support while his dad would've taken more convincing.

Doesn't matter now.

"What happened?" Brandon asked, but Owen refused to relay the story. There had been enough reminiscing this week, and his kiss with Lily came to mind. Hunching over at the wave of heat heading south to his groin, his mouth flattened into a foreboding line.

"Nothing that concerns you." Turning to his mother, he said, "Surely, they'll feel out of place among Society members and deal with a fair share of questioning looks."

"They're grown women who know how to handle themselves. They've done it well enough since the passing of their parents. A few haughty stares from the nobility won't phase them, I'm sure." Pausing, a shrewd expression appeared. "Is there a particular reason you don't want the Taylor sisters to attend?"

Yes, because one of them is the bane of my existence and a trap waiting for me to fall into headfirst.

"Not at all," he denied with a shrug. "If you want them to come, let them. It doesn't matter to me one way or the other."

Except I'll be sure to keep a healthy distance from them—or more specifically, the tall one with lithe curves and a temper to rival Artemis.

"WE LOOK RIDICULOUS." Lily paced across the room, accompanied by rustling from her taffeta skirt. The scarlet fabric resembled its richer cousin, silk, yet the shinier quality and distinct noise during movement declared its inferiority.

"Nonsense," Caraway said as she grabbed the matching reticule to her emerald gown. "We've removed unnecessary layers and slimmed it down in the front for the current style. No one will know the difference."

An unladylike snort came from Lily at the ridiculous statement. "These aren't common villagers like us. They're the nobility. It's written in their blood to notice the passé." She didn't mention how, even when the gowns were new nearly a decade ago that they still wouldn't have passed muster.

"I wish you wouldn't be so grim." Iris placed a beseeching hand on her arm as they waited for the Trent carriage to arrive. Lady Trent had graciously included the conveyance in her invitation. Otherwise, their old mare would've tugged them to the Trent estate in an open wagon.

Country bumpkins, indeed.

"While you may look like the fairy in Hazel's stories, you might remember you don't actually live in a children's tale." It vexed her how they tried to ignore their looming doom—as if pretending everything was sunshine and rainbows would make the problem with Laramie disappear.

She hated being the bearer of bad news, the one to point out their harsh reality all the time, and if it came out rude or blunt, it couldn't be helped. There were only so many times Lily could remind her sisters of the facts before it became ridiculous and increased her ire.

"Lily! Try to be kind," Caraway scolded. "Can't we agree to enjoy tonight? It's not often we get to attend such a lavish party."

Ironically, the last party they attended had been Hazel's wedding hosted by the Trents, and now they were headed back for another milestone celebration.

The jingle of carriage horses offered a reprieve from their argument, and they filed out of the cottage to meet the gleaming black conveyance with a golden crest on the side. A footman helped each of them into the velvety interior before the driver encouraged the horses forward at a sedate pace.

Torches lit the gravel drive lined with carriages of guests, and a knot formed in Lily's stomach. Setting aside her displeasure with Iris and Caraway, for the time being, her thoughts shifted. The opinions of society weighed less on her than the high possibility of seeing Owen. Their caustic departure the week prior would serve as an uncomfortable backdrop to the unavoidable meeting.

If you remain calm and collected, there'll be nothing to fear. He's hardly going to insult you in front of his mother and guests.

Moments later, they joined the receiving line to greet their hosts: the Dowager Countess and Earl of Trent. A task Lily wished they could skip.

"Good evening, my lord and my lady," Caraway said as the three women curtsied.

"Ah, Hampshire's Garden Girls... Isn't that what you call them, dear?" The dowager turned to her son with a playful swat of her fan. Diamonds glimmered at her ears and neck with the movement, and Lily felt the absence of their own elaborate jewelry keenly—a paste necklace weighing heavily around her neck. "Though we're missing young Hazel, aren't we? I would've adored hearing another one of her fantastical tales."

"Yes, responsibilities kept her and her husband in Manchester, I'm afraid. But we're hopeful for a visit soon."

"Ah, too bad. Their wedding was lovely, and I'd hoped to witness their marital bliss. Though, it *was* peculiar—the youngest sister married before the elder. But perhaps we can remedy that this evening." Her ladyship smiled encouragingly. "Plenty of available gentlemen in attendance for beautiful young women such as yourselves."

AN EARL LIKE ANY OTHER 41

"Mama..." Owen warned before facing them. His jacket buttons gleamed under the chandelier, punctuating the polished visage of a healthy young earl. From the top of his styled auburn hair to the shine on his shoes, he emanated wealth and superiority—a man confident in his worth and wasn't afraid to let everyone around him know it, either. "I apologize for my mother's impudent remarks. She has matrimony on her mind. It seems no one can escape it."

His gaze met Lily's with an unreadable expression, but it didn't surprise her that the dowager wanted Owen married off. All these years, she'd waited for the news of an engagement yet nothing, but that might change sooner rather than later as Lily studied the sparkling ladies around her. Her throat spasmed with a hard swallow as she swept an unsteady hand down the pale column. Owen's attention narrowed to the spot, riveted by the small act.

"No apology needed. We appreciate the suggestion," Iris said, her navy gown complementing the darker tones in her gray-blue eyes. "We're honored to be guests at such an auspicious event."

Lady Trent smiled at her enthusiasm, and Lily resisted a puff of disgruntlement. She absolutely would not be searching for a husband tonight. Especially not with the man who once frequented her girlish dreams in attendance.

After bidding the Trents adieu, they followed the crush of people towards a beautiful ballroom, a river of colorful fish waiting to be caught up in the sea of dancing and flirting—herself excluded, of course.

Planting her back to a wall, Lily observed the glittering crowd with a sigh of resignation and waited for the night to pass uneventfully. Iris and Cara could do as they wished, but she would not be lured into merriment.

Absolutely not.

CHAPTER FOUR

Unbeknownst to most, wallflowers had the best spot at parties. They could see everything that happened from a disguised vantage point behind potted plants or tall columns while hugging one of the four walls encasing them.

Which Lily realized too late as she watched Owen flirt with all the debutantes his mother paraded in front of him. Blonde, brunette, red-haired. A bevy of pretty young women suitable to make a match with an earl—unlike her.

And anger seethed in her veins, swirling with unrelenting jealousy.

I don't care what he does. He's free to do as he pleases.

She repeated the words over and over again, adding a tune to them at times, demanding that the lies become true. Their kiss must have snuck deeper under her skin than she'd realized if her blood was getting this worked up over silly flirtations.

I don't care. I don't care.

But an hour later when Owen made his way towards her, Lily straightened as an unbidden smoky wisp of hope blossomed in her chest. Would he ask her to dance?

"You've been watching me." A hard stare bore into her, and her shoulders slumped a degree before she remembered to compose herself.

"Have I? You think rather highly of yourself to presume such a thing." The snap of a fan sounded between them as she waved it over her flushing cheeks.

"I presume nothing. You don't think I know when your gaze follows me around the room?" Owen stepped closer, invading her space. "Trust me when I say I'm aware of your every movement."

A thrill swept through her blood at his clipped confession, satisfaction settling in her belly with the knowledge that he'd been as conscious of her as she'd been of him. Lords and ladies surrounded them, urging them closer together, and the fabric of Lily's dress scratched at her skin.

Lord, did he have to smell so delicious?

That accursed cinnamon tickled her nose again.

This is too much.

The people. The heat. Owen.

Multiplying emotions tugged her in every direction, and she needed to escape. Needed to redirect the evening—strengthen her resolve against him before she succumbed to his charms for the second time in two weeks.

"Think what you will," she said lamely. "I'm in need of fresh air." Lily dodged around him to weave through the ballroom until an exit appeared. Scurrying towards the open doorway, she passed through a smaller retiring room and kept going until the crowd thinned. The party confined to the east wing of the home, a sigh of relief fell from her lips as she took refuge in an empty room in the family quarters, though it didn't remain that way for long.

Owen trailed her like a hound on the hunt. When she dared look back on her mad escape, she'd witnessed a bevy

AN EARL LIKE ANY OTHER

of guests bombarding him, slowing his progress as he politely greeted them before pushing forward.

Not a minute later, the door slammed behind Owen, shutting out the faint noise of the ball and encapsulating them in a hush of anticipation.

The lock turned with a deafening click.

A portrait of his father glared down from a prominent position above the mantel as if scolding her for causing his son more trouble. Wooden chess pieces rested on a side table, prepared for game play, while leather-bound books filled a corner shelf.

Everything in its proper place. Except for her and Owen.

They shouldn't be alone. Forget her already-sullied reputation, capitulation concerned her more. Both of them giving in to the blaze sparking between them, the sure consequence whenever they argued.

Perhaps that's it.

Fire scorched through Lily's veins, searching for release, and her wild gaze caught on him, acknowledging the one way she could. They always fought, and it always ended in passion. It was a never-ending cycle.

But what if they completed the cycle? What if they finally surrendered to their desires, no holds barred?

She rushed up to him and started tugging at his clothes, moving to the waist of his trousers and fumbling with the buttons.

"Let's do this, here and now." The convoluted plan in her mind took root, its hazy edges ignored as she ached to reach some semblance of peace. To put right what she broke, even for a moment. Every black thought. Every bitter snap. They could be traced back to the day she decided to tear her and Owen apart.

Nothing had gone right since then, and nothing may go right again.

But at least they could have this evening and...

"Are you mad? We can't—" The interruption broke her unformed thought, bringing her back to the present.

"We can," she insisted, fighting his grip on her hands. "My reputation is ruined, you know this. Let's finally get this over with what we've wanted for years."

"What every man wants to hear from a woman: *let's get this over with*."

"Don't you want me?" She paused long enough to meet his gray gaze. "Don't lie, because if our kiss the other day is anything to go by, I know you do. And I want this, too. Maybe it'll burn out whatever lust still flames our blood."

Everyone already believed the worst of her, including Owen.

Why not steal a shred of pleasure from the man she wanted even as he infuriated her? She'd ruin herself for good now, and the gossip flying around the village would be a lie no longer.

His hand tangled in her hair and dragged her closer. "You truly believe such a thing is possible? One tup, and we won't feel this infernal draw towards each other?"

She didn't answer, just waited for him to make up his mind. She'd said all she could on the matter. For all their fighting, the time for talking had passed, and action was the name of the game tonight.

A groan emanated from him before he relented. "So be it, then."

AN EARL LIKE ANY OTHER

Victory.

He walked her backward until her back hit the wall with a thud and his mouth landed on hers in a rush of lust. Eagerly awaiting him, she resumed her attempts to remove his clothing as she reveled in his kiss. The ravenous nature echoed her own urgency as she finally met the bare skin of Owen's taut stomach—a mutual sound of pleasure passing between them at the contact.

Rough, biting nips traced down her neck and claimed her chest, the tops of her breasts blooming red beneath Owen's tongue and teeth. This differed from their trysts from before. They'd been hesitant, careful not to push the other too far.

Clearly, they were past such fear.

The rustle of bunched fabric incited Lily further as a cool breeze washed over her exposed legs. Owen shoved the mountain of skirts higher and brought a hand between quivering thighs to her core, and an unrepentant moan vibrated in her throat.

It had been so long since he'd touched her like this.

"Christ, you're already wet," he growled before deepening their kiss and starting to rub the bundle of nerves at the top of her sex between two fingers, surprising her with his memory of what pleased her.

"Is it any wonder?" Her breath caught at the building sensations centering in her quim. "We've spent years circling this moment like cats in heat. It's only natural for my body to respond in full approval of our long-awaited joining."

"And we shan't wait any longer."

Lily watched beneath slitted lashes as he released his engorged member from its confines and fit himself between her legs. A shadow of doubt passed over her—a worry that perhaps she should tell him the truth first—but it became too late when he pushed inside, and a cry of pain echoed in the room as she tensed at the breach.

Owen stopped immediately, a horrified look of knowledge dawning. "You're a virgin?"

He tried jerking away, but she held tight to him, determined even as tears formed. "Just finish it." She needed this completion. The pain would stop. Even now it ebbed to a dull ache, but things between them would still balance on a pin needle and she needed them to fall one way or the other.

Please, finish it.

Her heart throbbed—begged—for completion.

Wresting her hands from his waist, Owen stepped back, and she flinched at the emptiness he left behind. "Why would you... How could you let me...?" He tucked himself back into his trousers and began pacing around the room, a shaky hand ruffling his hair.

"How could you do this? Our first time together and this? Frenzied, passionate, I could handle. But for you to..." An agitated arm swept out and a cream vase full of roses careened towards the carpet, shattering.

Lily jumped at the muted crash as shards of ceramic scattered on the floor. "It's done now," she said numbly, brushing at her skirts in a hopeless effort to smooth out the wrinkles. Unfortunately, taffeta didn't smooth out.

And neither did the lingering effects of desire clinging to her body.

Or the wash of heartache besieging her soul.

Disbelieving eyes speared her to the wall. "Done? It's only bloody begun. We'll need to marry now."

Incredulous laughter burbled up. *Perhaps hysterical?* "Now, who's mad? I'm not marrying you. I'm not marrying anyone. It's entirely unnecessary. No one knows what we've done, and if they did, it's not like I can be ruined twice."

At least her brain function seemed to be returning. That last point seemed rather clever.

"*I* know what I've done, and I take responsibility for my part in this farce." He stalked nearer though kept a respectable distance as if he couldn't bear risking a touch. "You will marry me, Lily Taylor, and you will be the next Countess of Trent."

"Never." She shook her head, which set the flood of waiting tears free. Wiping a hand over her cheeks, she weakly repeated the promise. "Never."

Whipping around, she struggled with the locked door before flipping the latch and fleeing the room, crushing her skirts in a sweaty grip as she ran down the hall, frantic gaze searching for a way out. *Think, Lily*. She envisioned past visits to the Trent home—elaborate games of hide and seek with her sisters and Owen—until a vague map arose, and she followed defining landmarks—plum drapes with fringe along the bottom which she'd loved to comb her fingers through, an elaborate peacock planter housing large leafy fronds.

Soon, her memory proved reliable when gardens appeared through a closed set of French doors, and Lily eased past the unlocked barrier into a wonderland of color highlighted by moonlight.

Leave it for Owen to notify her abandoned sisters of her departure.

Lily gulped in the fresh air before removing her slippers and taking off at a sprint home. A miracle feat considering the layers of fabric weighing her down.

Owen.

If she couldn't marry him at eighteen, she most certainly couldn't marry him at twenty-five! The reasons they shouldn't remained as tall and foreboding as Mount Everest.

He's noble; she's not.

He's respectable; she's a ruined woman.

And a whole host of other reasons she'd written down all those years ago. She just needed to find that list again.

When the cottage rose to the forefront, Lily added one last burst of speed and hurried inside before collapsing on the wooden floor, struggling for breath. A scream stuck in her throat. She wished she could rid herself of the roiling darkness sweeping through her, but it was there to stay—a part of her now.

Hiccupping gasps filled the room as salty tears tracked down her cheeks. Soon, she'd need to escape upstairs before her sisters returned to find her in a sniveling heap. Answering inquiries about her disappearance from the ball would be too much for her.

A vague explanation would come tomorrow. Until then she wanted to be alone.

Forever alone.

Well and truly now.

A VIRGIN!

Disbelief radiated from his pores.

A fucking virgin.

That incredible fact bounced around in his addled brain. All these years she'd let him believe—let everyone believe—Lynch's claims of her lost virtue, yet they'd obviously been false.

Sinking into a leather chair, Owen hung his head in shame, even though fury raged in his blood. It was an odd combination that made him sick to his stomach.

They'd waited all this time, and to finally consummate their relationship in such a horrid way tore at him. Two virgins no longer.

And throughout all of it, a spark of hope sprouted deep inside his soul. He didn't know why she'd lied for so long, but Lily wasn't immune to him. Tonight proved a modicum of feelings on her part. Perhaps they could start again. After all, he couldn't let her act as if their joining never happened. They must marry.

But she lied. And she did kiss Lynch. You saw it.

Yes, he did.

Owen would have to get to the bottom of why she betrayed him in such a way, but kiss or not—ruined or not—he'd have her as his wife.

Who she was always meant to be.

Passing conversation in the hall filtered into the room, and he knew it was time to return to the ball. Standing to his feet, a neutral expression on his face, he started to leave when the broken vase caught his eye, recalling his outburst with guilt. He'd need to send a servant in to clean it up before someone injured themselves.

After mentioning the mess to a maid, he rejoined the party and made his way to Caraway and Iris, who stood like wallflowers, hugging the edges of the ballroom.

"Where have you been? Have you seen Lily? We seem to have lost her." Caraway searched the ballroom for her wayward sister, her heels lifted off the floor to help her small stature see through the crowd.

"She went home," he explained, avoiding her gaze. "She wasn't feeling well."

"Oh, dear. I hope it's not serious like one of her migraines. Perhaps we should leave." Iris wrung her hands in concern.

Her odd statement confused him—*one of her migraines*. The Lily he'd known exuded an aura of health, never ill, and a change in that assessment troubled him.

"No, you must stay; she doesn't want you to worry."

"I'm surprised she chose to confide in you." Caraway turned speculative eyes on him, and he felt like one of those plants their father used to study under the microscope.

"It was less of a confidence rather than an opportunity to relay the message before leaving. If not me, it would've been a servant, I'm sure." He brushed over the speculation before she could dive too deeply. It wouldn't do to share anything about his and Lily's scandalous encounter. He'd deal with her privately.

Catching his mother holding court across the room, Owen dipped his head in farewell. "I must see to the guest of honor. If I don't see you again tonight, I hope you enjoy the evening."

"Thank you, and good luck." Caraway glanced over his shoulder. "She seemed quite keen on a match for you."

"Try as she might, I won't be marrying until I'm ready."

Which will be fairly soon.

Lily would not escape his grasp, and the irony wasn't lost on him.

An earl didn't chase; women sought him.

Yet he intended to chase Lily Taylor—he would not give her up again.

CHAPTER FIVE

"Mr. Laramie is here," Cara said from the window, spying the man exiting a carriage stopped in front of their cottage. Clouds blanketed the sky in gray, and Lily prayed it would drench him in a sudden downpour rivaling the one that sent Noah's ark floating around the world. She could use a bit of cheer after a week spent avoiding Owen and all thoughts of him. *Not very successfully, though.*

He crept into her dreams without warning, their evening together morphing into one of continued pleasure rather than the catastrophe of reality.

"But...we have one more day." Iris's light brows wrinkled in worry at the hurried end to Laramie's timeline.

"Would it really make a difference?" Lily asked, noting the frustratingly dry weather outside. For the past two weeks, they had worked hard to follow through on Cara's foolhardy plan of creating the book themselves, but it was no use.

They weren't their father or mother. They didn't have the skills or knowledge to compile an in-depth book of research on moss. *Thwarted by a bloody plant.*

"Well, he's here. Early or not, we're going to have to give him what we have."

"Which is nothing." Scoffing, Lily sat in her father's favorite chair, crossed arms matching her crossed legs with calves encased in breeches from her earlier outdoor meanderings. She hadn't wanted to change, and now it seemed Laramie would catch her in such an unladylike repose—again.

No matter, she thought. What did she care what he thought of her manners when he was kicking her family out of their home without a second thought? Politeness clearly wasn't in his repertoire, so it wouldn't be in hers.

An imperious knock rapped against the door, and Lily inhaled a breath of preparation for what was to come.

"Mr. Laramie." Caraway greeted him with a grim smile. "What a surprise to see you so soon. I thought we had until tomorrow for your proposition."

"You're not mistaken, Miss Taylor. However, I arrived early in the village and figured we should get this nasty bit of business over with. Have you obtained the payment?"

Lily tried hiding her disgust. Of course, his immediate concern was jumping right to the topic of money.

"Why don't you have a seat?" Caraway gestured to an armchair across from Lily. "And maybe some tea?"

Mr. Laramie held up a placating hand, and she noted another peculiar brown spot on the back of it, one to match the one she'd seen on his first visit. "I'm afraid I prefer a quick visit, thank you."

"Why the haste, Mr. Laramie?" Iris asked. "Do you have other plans while visiting the countryside?"

"Hardly." Disapproval rang in his tone. "After my travels abroad, I prefer London these days instead of rustic communities."

He made it sound like they were backwoods Neanderthals instead of a perfectly charming English village. One Lily sometimes resented after her scandal, but the rolling hills and forests made up for the lapse.

"I see." Caraway sat next to Iris on the settee, her hands clasped in her lap. "To the point, Mr. Laramie, I fear we have not been able to gather enough funds to cover our father's contract with you. However, if you could only—"

"I thought as much, which is why a new plan occurred to me."

This couldn't bode well for them. What other plan could he possibly contrive? They either had the money or not and clearly, they did not.

"Oh?" Iris leaned forward, light blonde wisps falling over her shoulder.

"I've been thinking... I'm not getting any younger. I'd like to leave more than my work behind when I pass." He paused and Lily felt his gaze travel over her, pausing on her trouser-clad legs. For the second time, she regretted not changing and felt out of place wearing breeches instead of her dresses. The way he ogled her made the hair on the back of her nape rise in warning.

"It occurred to me that if you don't have the money to offer, you still have something else of equal or greater value." A pit formed in Lily's stomach as she raced to work out his meaning. Something of equal or greater value? Did he want to buy what's left of her father's supplies? Journals?

"And what would that be, Mr. Laramie?" Cara asked, a worried note entering her voice.

"I am in need of a wife to birth my children, and while it might be customary for me to marry the eldest..." He glanced at Cara. "I would prefer to have someone more to my tastes.

A hearty country girl who can withstand the elements of wherever we may travel."

Lily understood where this was leading, as no one had ever described Iris as hardy, not with her fae-like aura. Cara must have worked out what he meant, too, because mutual expressions of shock bounced between the two of them. "You can't be serious."

"What? You'd prefer to lose your childhood home? I'm not being unreasonable. You owe me a debt. This way benefits everyone. I've heard the talk at the inn about Miss Lily's exploits in her youth, and I'm willing to overlook them. You won't be getting a better offer than that."

That's it.

She'd had enough.

Jumping to her feet, Lily straightened to her full height. "I will never marry you." And a sense of deja vu almost made her dizzy as she remembered uttering the same phrase to Owen five days prior.

"I think you will, my dear. It's either marriage to me, with a hope for a future family, your home safe and sound for your sisters, or the three of you out on the streets."

"You are a vile man." Like a feral cat, she wanted to hiss and bite the odious man. How dare he try to blackmail her into marriage! "What a proposal—or shall I say threat—you make to the woman you hope to be your bride. Is it any wonder I refuse you?"

She'd refused Owen, a man she'd once loved. Hell would freeze over before she agreed to become *this* man's wife, instead. Lightning bolted through her bones, down to the very tips of her fingers, and she wished she could blast Laramie to ash.

"I've upset you," Laramie said, lifting to his feet, acting as if her rage wasn't threatening to pummel him into the ground. "You have until I leave Hampshire tomorrow morning. I'll stop here before proceeding to London. If you insist on refusing my hand, then I'm afraid I'll have no choice but to move forward with legal proceedings and take ownership of this land and home."

"We quite understand what's at stake." Cara moved to the door, forcefully swinging it open. "You will have your answer by then. Now if you will excuse us, we have a lot to discuss."

He left, leaving them in a wake of disbelief, or in Lily's case, fury. The only silver lining was the heavens opening up in a deluge of rain right over Laramie's thick skull.

The rest of the afternoon and evening was spent agonizing over what to do next. Should they write to Hazel and Jonathan? Try reasoning with Mr. Laramie again? The one option they didn't consider—to Lily's relief—was Mr. Laramie's proposal.

However, privately, as hours passed with no better solutions found, she knew what had to be done to save her family home, and the knowledge chafed.

Her sisters wouldn't accept financial aid from Owen. Wouldn't want to be seen as taking advantage of his friendship. Especially since Lily doubted he'd allow them to repay the debt to him instead.

And while the idea of Owen frightening Mr. Laramie off gave her an unladylike sort of pleasure, it wasn't a permanent solution because the contract still legally bound them to him.

Which left one option—one her sisters and Mr. Laramie couldn't circumvent or deny.

She'd visit Owen and accept his proposal. *If he still wants you.* But she knew he would. His sense of duty wouldn't let him do anything less.

Against all odds, they'd marry in the end.

Despite the ruining of her reputation in an effort to push him away.

Despite the distrust she'd placed between them.

And bitterness gnawed at her insides.

THE NEXT MORNING BEFORE Laramie's purported return, Lily donned her favorite gown, a light blue muslin with sprigged daisies dotting the fabric, needing the strength and confidence it imbued. She'd spent the entire night debating how to approach Owen, which culminated in purple circles under her eyes, an attractive feature in a future bride, no doubt. However, nothing could be done about it now.

His lordship would have to learn to accept her in all capacities anyway, whether fatigued from a sleepless evening or outfitted for tea with the queen.

Sneaking downstairs with tentative steps, Lily strained to hear the telltale patter of her sisters' morning routine. Silence greeted her, and the tense muscles along her neck and shoulders marginally relaxed. Cara and Iris must be on their morning walk. Thankful for her good fortune, she hurried downstairs, grabbed her bonnet from a hook by the door, and began the trek towards the Trent Estate.

Though it was too early for proper visiting hours, she knew Owen would see her. How could he resist the opportunity when they hadn't spoken since the night of his mother's ball? Curiosity would be too great a temptress.

A quarter of an hour later, Lily stood in a room Marvin the butler had reluctantly deposited her in, the soothing green tones doing nothing to ease her nerves. Chaotic energy tingled from her booted toes to gloved fingertips, and she reconsidered the approach she'd settled on sometime in the night. Perhaps sticking to the blunt route of their past interactions wasn't wise. What's that saying about catching more flies with honey?

Except Owen would see through such a ruse, as he'd always been able to glean her true feelings. *The blighter.* It was unfair how attuned he'd always been to her, even if she felt the same could be said for her in regard to him… At least she used to be.

Only time would tell now.

Time spent together as husband and wife if he accepted her proposition.

CHAPTER SIX

Our lips touched for the first time in years, and I confess confusion. Oh, my love, why must things always be so difficult?

HOW DID FATHER DO IT?

Piles of paperwork lay before Owen, and he failed to fathom how his father managed it all himself. Owen's grandfather certainly hadn't known one end of a plow from the other. His focus was turned towards leisurely pursuits which emptied the family coffers. Which led his father to Ireland and his future wife. Neither of which offered insight into farming knowledge or tenant management.

Years of tutelage at school and under his father's care seemed for naught as he struggled to balance everything.

Banging his head against the back of the chair, Owen scrubbed his cheeks in temporary defeat and moved on to another pressing matter: Lily.

Was it fair to blame her for his lack of motivation? His thoughts rang constantly with memories of her—old and new.

Almost a week, and nary a peep from her.

He'd visited her cottage and learned she was jaunting about the lake. Except he hadn't found her after searching the usual paths.

When he'd returned again, Iris had informed him that Lily wasn't feeling well, so couldn't accept visitors.

He'd even left a note in their old hiding spot at the lake requesting—well, demanding—a meeting. *Lot of good that did me.* The folded sheet of paper remained unmoved last he checked.

"Pardon me, my lord, but Miss Lily Taylor is here to see you. I've put her in the green drawing-room." *Speak of the devil...* Perhaps, she had read his letter.

"Thank you, Marvin." Crossing the hall towards the aforementioned room, Owen halted at the closed door, his hand wavering over the knob. Which Lily awaited him? The girl of his youth finally come to her senses? Or the woman who'd orchestrated their disastrous coupling?

Could she be pregnant? Though it'd be an exceedingly rare case, considering he hadn't—ahem, *finished*—inside her, it wasn't completely unheard of.

Don't be an idiot. It's impossible to know so soon.

Right, shaking his head of any more ridiculous musings and steeling his spine, Owen casually opened the door, affecting a nonchalance he was far from feeling.

"What a pleasant surprise..."

She stood tall and proud in a pretty gown that highlighted her figure. Strong and capable with the perfect amount of curves, he admitted privately that he'd never met a woman who could compare to her. "I didn't expect you to willingly grace my doorstep again after your committed avoidance this week. To what do I owe the pleasure?"

Say you'll marry me.

"I've come to accept your proposal under one condition."

AN EARL LIKE ANY OTHER

"Name it."

Lifting her chin to an obstinate angle, she met his determined gaze with a bold one of her own. "You must pay off my father's debt, specifically to a Mr. Edward Laramie. He claims my father owes him for an incomplete research project and is threatening to take the land and cottage for recompense."

"I see." Hands clasped behind his back, Owen walked closer to Lily's position at the center of the room. His leisurely strides belied any outward reaction to the news, as did the composed expression he maintained. "I suppose it's some relief you haven't lost all of your good sense—choosing to come to me to save your sisters, if not yourself. I accept your terms."

Releasing a pent-up breath, a satisfied grin almost emerged at her victory, and it amused him since he felt victorious as well. Saving her family from disaster was a small price to pay to get what he wanted.

Her.

"Excellent. Now, come with me." She crossed the room with long, purposeful strides before grabbing his hand and hauling him along behind her.

It was inappropriate. Unladylike. And the servants they passed in the hall were sure to gossip about it until sundown.

But he couldn't care less. Inciting, then weathering, gossip seemed to be her specialty. Besides, soon they'd be referring to her as "my lady", and all the tittle-tattle would increase tenfold. No use bothering with proprieties now.

"Where are we going?" Owen asked, heels digging into the carpet to stop her rush forward. There were details needing to be discussed. Foremost in his mind, why the devil she'd kissed

Asa Lynch seven years ago? Why she let him believe the worst of her for so long?

Owen accepted his need for her, but his trust wasn't so easily restored.

"To tell my sisters the good news."

"And it has to be this very moment?"

"Yes."

Time was, apparently, of the essence. Chuckling at the vast switch from her previous lackadaisical reaction to his proposal, he added more of his weight to her hold on him, slowing her down even more.

"How quickly can your carriage be ready? Or perhaps we should walk to save time. Though arriving in a noble carriage would certainly make a statement." He didn't think that last part was spoken to him. She seemed to be running through scenarios in her head. What for, he hadn't a clue.

Tired of indulging her, Owen came to a stop on the stone steps outside, tugging Lily backward before she tumbled down to the gravel drive. "Slow down." A huff of exasperation burst forth as she yanked out of his grip. "We'll ride in the carriage, and you can explain the haste."

"Very well." Arms crossing over her heaving chest, she caught his surreptitious glance downward before his eyes fastened on hers. A becoming flush rose to her skin at his perusal, and he dared to look again, a wicked grin lifting the corners of his mouth.

"You are insufferable. We're not married yet." But her words held no heat, only a breathy tone that wrapped around his cock and squeezed.

"No, but we will be. And it's not as if I haven't sampled those particular charms of yours before." *And how sweet they'd been.* He'd relish the moment she belonged to him completely, when there was no longer a need to meet in secret or hide their desire.

Their wedding couldn't come soon enough.

WHILE LILY STOOD LIKE a moon-eyed calf, mouth hanging half-open at Owen's indecent reminder, he called for Marvin and ordered his horse and carriage to be brought around. She hadn't expected him to blatantly flirt with her. The last time they'd been in each other's company he'd been furious.

And now, he acted as if the past didn't matter to him—well, the negative bits at least—as she recalled his comment about her breasts.

When two chestnut horses trotted up to the main entrance, they settled on opposite sides of the conveyance, while Lily relayed the woeful predicament the Taylor sisters found themselves in—skipping over Laramie's marriage proposal to her. She didn't think he'd like hearing how she'd been willing to lose her family home if need be, but becoming Laramie's wife was a step too far.

That being Owen's countess resided below living on the street.

You wouldn't have ended up in the street. You would've been homeless, not penniless.

When they stopped in front of the cottage, Lily smiled at seeing Mr. Laramie's hired coach present.

Perfect.

"A bit early for company, isn't it?"

"The man's like a dog with a bone." Lily landed on the ground with a slight thump, ignoring Owen's offer of help. "Shall we save Cara and Iris from his greedy clutches?"

Not waiting for an answer, she practically ran down the stone path leading to the cottage entrance, whipping the door open to a stunned audience. Owen entered without ceremony, but with no less surprise from the three people standing before them.

"Mr. Laramie, how fortunate you're here! It means we can end this bad business once and for all."

"Lily..." Caraway gave a minute shake of her head, a hard stare boring into her reckless sister.

Ignoring the warning, Lily continued, overwhelmed with her success and eager to send Laramie back from whence he came. "I'm afraid I must refuse your proposal, as I'm already betrothed to this man, the Earl of Trent. He's also agreed to take care of what we owe for our father's breached contract." Owen's body straightened to attention—no, he didn't like hearing this newest tidbit.

"Betrothed!"

"When did this happen?"

Multiple exclamations spouted from around the room, but none more volcanic than from Mr. Laramie. "This is outrageous!" Wagging a finger in her direction, his eyes bulged from their sockets as he continued to bluster in fury. "You little hoyden! You think you can thwart me with this fraud?"

He motioned to Owen in disgust, and it occurred to her that he genuinely didn't recognize a man of quality when presented with one. A mocking laugh mounted in her chest. "I

AN EARL LIKE ANY OTHER

assure you, sir. This is the Earl of Trent, and I am his betrothed. With our debt soon to be settled, I believe it's time for you to leave. I'd wish you a good day, but hoydens aren't known for their manners."

A sweetly taunting smile edged Lily's lips, which she could admit might have exacerbated the situation when Laramie charged forward like a bull seeing red. Frozen in place, her legs morphed into pillars of marble as Laramie's angry form loomed large, the concerned cries of her sisters echoing in her ears.

Suddenly, the image disappeared.

The tall shadow of Owen fell upon her—shoulders rigid, muscles taut. He stood between Lily and Laramie, a protective wall of lethal intensity. "Lay a hand on my future wife—the future Countess of Trent—and I will see you jailed before the sun sets this eve. Cast any more aspersions on her character, and you will find yourself lying on the ground, short a functioning jaw to speak. Do I make myself clear?"

A tremor of heat slid down her spine, like a dollop of honey melting over a warm biscuit, except the weakening in her resolve to remain immune to him didn't sit nearly as sweetly in her mind as it did her heart.

Laramie paused his aggressive stride, sputtering nonsense until he composed himself enough to murmur, "Apologies, my lord. The notion that a man such as yourself would marry a common country girl... Well, you can see why I doubted Miss Lily's assertion."

"The Taylor women are dear friends of my family and under our protection. With my marriage to Miss Lily, it will be doubly true. My solicitor will contact you about settling Mr. Taylor's debt; a copy of the contract will be requested to attest to your claim. Until then, I believe Miss Lily had the right of it. Our business is concluded, and it's time for you to go."

The cheerful chirping of meadowlarks filtered through the window as they waited for Laramie's reaction in the ensuing silence. Surely, he wouldn't risk furthering an earl's ire by refusing Owen's command.

"Indeed." Bending into a quick bow, Laramie swept a hand across his sweaty forehead, the edges of a dark spot peeking out at his hairline, before heading towards the doorway. Owen sidestepped out of the man's way, careful to keep his body between Laramie and Lily. "I'll await your solicitor's correspondence in London. Good day, sir... ladies." The last word dripped with sarcastic doubt as he shot one last beady glare at Lily before finally making his exit.

A tense lull coated the room before it exploded into incredulous voices clamoring for an explanation, and Lily's ears rang with admonishments. She'd saved her family from being cast out of their childhood home, yet this was the thanks she received? Was it too much to hope for an expression of gratitude rather than reprimands?

The black pit always hovering in the background flared to life—a stark reminder of how unfairly life treated her. How even when she tried to do good, it ended badly.

"Would someone care to explain how the two of you jumped from avoiding each other to betrothed in the span of a few weeks?" Caraway's pointed question directed itself towards Lily.

"Feelings changed after my mother's ball. Lily and I were able to discuss the past, and events progressed from there."

A half-truth.

AN EARL LIKE ANY OTHER

She didn't recall much of a discussion outside of Owen's shouting after breaching her maidenhead.

"How convenient... After years of discord, one reunited evening erases the past and lands you an engagement." Cara studied Lily's face, searching for clues as to the real story behind the abrupt change. It was no secret the animosity Lily held for Owen after the scandal. "An engagement arriving in the nick of time to save our family from disaster at the hands of Mr. Laramie. Remarkable!"

"Oh, stop being so cynical, Cara." Iris cut in with a reassuring pat to her sister's crossed arms before gliding forward, arms outstretched to hug Lily. "I'm happy to hear you've worked through your troubles, dear. And such a romantic tale! Falling in love across a ballroom floor, a second chance at happiness." She turned to Owen and embraced him just as strongly.

Lily tamped down an answering jeer at the fairy tale embellishment of that night; no use disabusing her sisters of the ridiculous notion. Perhaps it would win a quicker acceptance of the news since she didn't fancy an interrogation.

One can dream.

"Does your mother know?" This time, the dart plunged into Owen's armor as he winced at Cara's question. Dear lord, she'd forgotten about the dowager countess. How would she feel about gaining a daughter-in-law with a less-than-perfect pedigree?

She's Irish. She can't be too harsh on you.

But a niggling doubt persisted.

"LADIES, FIRST." OWEN motioned for Lily to enter the sitting room before him, but she hesitated, sudden apprehension wrinkling her dark brows. "What? Don't tell me you've lost your nerve? After dragging me across Shoreham for the performance of a lifetime in front of your Mr. Laramie?"

Caraway and Iris's interrogation over the surprise engagement had spanned an hour's time, and now they prepared themselves to answer more inquiries from his mother back at the Trent home. At this point, he almost wished Lily had dragged his mother along with them to the Taylor cottage earlier, just to avoid reiterating the tale.

"He's not *my* anything. I made sure of that by proposing to you, didn't I?" Lily's ungloved hands clasped and unclasped, and tugged at her sleeve cuffs, before returning to their earlier position. The unusual fidgeting reminded Owen how much time had passed since he'd truly known her. The girl he used to know burst with energy, true, but it was always directed towards accomplishing one thing or another. Never had he seen her restless with anxiety.

And the change endeared him more towards her.

Gather yourself. One chink in her armor isn't cause to become a lovesick puppy again. Especially without a proper explanation about Lynch.

"Yes, a rather Cornelian dilemma. Either choice would've been terrible in your mind, I suspect." And it irritated him to no end. Did she really think so little of him? They both maintained their reservations about the other. But to place him in a category so close to that bastard Laramie?

It wasn't right.

Before she could form a rebuttal, the amused melody of his mother's voice drifted over them. "Are you two planning on spending all afternoon arguing in the hall, or will you finally grace me with your presence?"

Lily's cheeks flushed a deep scarlet, and he feared his own face held the same look of embarrassment at the gentle chastisement. His arm waved forward once again—daring her to deny him a second time, now that they were aware of their audience—before following her inside to share the news of their impending nuptials. No doubt his mother would be thrilled.

The dowager countess lounged regally in her favorite spot by the bay windows, the picture of noble gentility and grace, her flame-red tresses the only outward sign of a rebellious streak that ran through her veins. Courtesy of an Irish grandmother, of course. A leather-bound book lay in one hand while the other placed an emerald ribbon between the pages to mark her spot.

He waited for Lily to be seated before joining her on the settee; their close proximity stiffening her shoulders. *How flattering.* Every man wanted his future bride to go stiff as a floorboard in his presence. Stifling a bemused cough, Owen waited for his mother's opening volley.

"I take it you have something of importance to share with me?"

"It seems you shall have your birthday wish, after all, Mama. Miss Lily and I are to be wed."

An expressive brow arched in surprise, though he saw the twitch of a smile toying around his mother's mouth. She was pleased with the news. *She's always liked Lily...*

"What a splendid development!" Clapping her hands together in approval, Lady Trent nonetheless speared Owen with a look of reprisal. "However, I don't recall you asking for your grandmama's ring. Did you propose to this lovely girl without it?"

Damn, he'd forgotten about the ring. Since he was a boy, his mother had shared the story of her Irish origins and the antique ring handed down from generation to generation. No matter the family's circumstances—rich or poor—the ring stood the test of time.

But he could hardly be blamed for the oversight. Both proposals were hasty and precipitated by life-altering events. Didn't leave much time to race down to the family jewels.

"At the risk of sounding ill-bred, I'm afraid I proposed to your son, my lady. So, the absence of the ring is entirely my fault." Lily stepped in, shocking him with her defense. He thought she might have let him bear the brunt of his mother's reprisal or join his mother's light teasing.

"A modern woman! Just what the next Countess of Trent should be." Reaching to tap Lily's arm in affection, his mother smiled in easy acceptance of Lily's brazen admission. "Welcome to the family, dear. Though, I suppose, you and your sisters have always been part of it as much as you children played together. But it will be good to make it official. We shall start wedding planning immediately. When can your sisters join us to help?"

Owen drifted off during the rest of the conversation as it shifted to wedding fripperies and the like. Gaze drawn to the portrait of his father hanging above the mantel, a portion of his mother's words nagged at him.

You've always been part of our family.

A long-forgotten conversation with his father played in his mind's eye, replacing the sunlit drawing room with the darker tones of the former earl's study. After his twentieth birthday celebration, Father had invited Owen to the familiar room for a serious discussion about his future. Raised from an early age to learn the inner workings of the estate—more so than even his peers, who relied on managers—Owen knew his future duty to the land and tenants.

But his father had wanted to discuss a different topic altogether: that of marriage and heirs.

"Son, I've seen the way you look at the Taylor girl, witnessed the fiery exchanges between you two." Reclining behind his desk, the earl addressed Owen with kindness tempered by an iron determination. "That girl's a wild filly; the whole family embodies a sort of peculiarity."

Owen prepared to defend them, but Father lifted a staying hand. "I mean no offense. I like them; we're not exactly known for our conventionality either, are we? Not with your dear mother's Irish blood." He sighed in resignation, and Owen recalled the necessity of his parents' marriage. How the earldom had been near destitute when Father had traveled to Ireland on a tip from a friend about a speculation opportunity. While the opportunity fell through, the luck of the Irish hadn't deserted him. Instead, the earl met a wealthy distiller's daughter and a match was struck.

However mercenary the tale, Owen knew his parents loved each other, and he hoped to emulate their marriage to his own children.

"What I'm trying to say is think about the path you're on. The past two generations of Trents have made a bungle of our legacy.

First, your grandfather gambling away our fortune, thus forcing me to marry a woman below my station in order to restore said fortune. No offense to your mother, of course, but facts are facts. I care about your happiness, and I know you believe it lies with Miss Lily, but would you condemn your heirs to another mark against their lineage?"

"You act as if my life has been ruined by our family's past. As if a couple of side glances from uppity matrons matters to me. I love Lily like you love Mama, and we'll handle any negative gossip together." A fierce light glowed in Owen's eyes, his father's crestfallen expression doing nothing to dim it.

"I was afraid this would be your response." Father shook his head in sadness, but didn't forbid Owen from seeing Lily again. "You can be bull-headed when you want to be, but you're a man now, which means you'll need to learn through experience."

And, by Jove, had he learned.

"My dear, are you listening?" Mama asked, shattering the past memory. Lily and she looked expectantly at him, and he struggled to return to the present.

His father had warned him about choosing Lily. Yet, he'd done so anyway, and she betrayed him. Perhaps not in the way he'd thought, but the kiss he'd witnessed between her and Lynch hadn't been an illusion.

Now, he was choosing her again, and a sense of foreboding settled like a pall over his thoughts. What would his decision bring about this time?

CHAPTER SEVEN

We're betrothed! After everything we've been through, I can hardly believe it! There's so much left to discuss... But for now, I'll leave you with a kiss until we're together again.
All my love...

AFTER SETTLING ON A wedding date three months hence, Owen's mother insisted on purchasing Lily's trousseau and new gowns for her sisters as a wedding gift. Thus, she found herself standing in a London modiste's one month later, arms akimbo as a miniature woman scrambled around Lily, taking a plethora of measurements.

"My lady, I must reiterate how unnecessary this extravagant expense is. I'm perfectly content wearing my mother's dress for the occasion."

"Not the one your younger sister already wore for her own wedding?" Owen's mother, Lady Trent, waved a bejeweled hand in the air. "I appreciate sentimentality, but I can't in good conscience let you walk down St. George's in a twice-worn hand-me-down. You'll be much more comfortable in a gown exuding the latest style trends, made especially for you, dear."

"Mais oui," the French modiste inserted. "You will be the most fashionable bride of the Season."

"Oh, imagine the expressions of awe you'll elicit!" Iris stared dreamily at the bolt of cream silk appointed for the wedding gown. "A country girl marrying an earl of the realm; you'll be like Cinderella!"

"Let's hope I don't turn into a pumpkin..." Lily quipped, flinching at a sharp poke to her ribs where Mrs. Fleur began draping muslin into a suitable shape.

"No pumpkins. You must retain this lovely figure for your gown."

"I wouldn't worry about Miss Lily increasing, madam." Caraway lifted her head from the book of patterns she'd been perusing. "She's quite athletic. In fact, I believe she could outrun many of the lords we've seen bandying about town since our arrival in London."

Lily almost thought she detected a note of pride in her sister's voice. *Absurd.* Cara lived by a code of propriety and responsibility to her family. The very idea that she'd approve of Lily's unique ability bucked her sense of what was proper.

A good English girl did not run or race. She walked sedately. And she most assuredly did not compete against men, let alone blue bloods.

Lady Trent nodded in agreement. "Yes, you and my son have that in common: you're both enormously active people, even if his preference is swimming rather than sticking to dry land."

Lily ducked her head to hide an unexpected blush. Owen swimming in the lake. Her catching him shirtless, tan skin glistening with fresh drops of water.

She remembered the thirst parching her throat that particular morning years ago and forced a harsh swallow to alleviate the sudden dryness pervading now.

Stop thinking about him!

Animated chatter continued around the small parlor as she berated herself for her foolish, wayward thoughts—and the frustrating reaction in her body. It'd been years since she'd felt attraction for a man, and for it to reappear for the same man at such inopportune times was frustrating in the extreme.

You'll need to get used to it eventually. Especially since your wedding night is only a few short months away.

To be honest, she hadn't a clue what to expect on that auspicious evening. Would they pretend to be like a normal couple and officially consummate their joining? Should she even want such a thing?

They still hadn't discussed the past. She knew he had questions, and frankly, she harbored doubts about him. The ease with which he judged her and believed the worst didn't sit well. Their foundation of trust lay in a pile of rubble that seemed unsalvageable most of the time.

"Could we have a word in private, dears? Before Madame Fleur returns?" Iris and Cara nodded before departing the dressing room, leaving the Lily and Owen's mother alone after the modiste went to the back for more pins.

Lily fumbled with the ring on her finger, Owen's grandmother's ring. Sweat made the silver slide easily over the thin skin.

What could Lady Trent have to say that required privacy?

"We haven't had a moment to ourselves yet, so I wanted to take the opportunity to say how happy I am that you and my

Owen are marrying. I've always sensed a connection between you, even during the horrid time with that stable boy. Whatever happened doesn't matter to me, though I tend to lean more towards believing your side of the story if you ever feel compelled to share it with me." Another gentle lifting of Lady Trent's lips met Lily's befuddled gaze. When had she secured the countess's approval and trust? *How* had she secured it?

"My son has wandered aimlessly for years now. It's a shame his father's death coincided with your ordeal. I fear it became too much for him, so he left. But I don't think he ever found the peace he searched for. I'm hoping you can bring him that peace as the two of you start anew. Hopefully wiser as adults than you were as youths, hmm?"

Fear rose like a beast hiding underneath a child's bed.

She couldn't bring peace to Owen. She couldn't even bring it to herself.

And as far as wisdom... Their escapade at the lady's birthday ball crushed that hope.

Swiping at a bead of sweat on her forehead, Lily muttered a semblance of agreement before Madame Fleur returned to save her. In a flash of clarity, it became obvious that the shadow lurking inside her would follow her into marriage. Would taint Owen, as well. The tendrils of it had already seeped into his life by forcing them to marry due to fate's vendetta against her.

As if I haven't already cast enough trouble on his life.

A lump lodged in her throat as a filmy haze of tears clouded her sight. He'd be stuck with her forever.

Stuck in the sticky muck of anger and bitterness and misfortune she couldn't seem to detach herself from.

AN EARL LIKE ANY OTHER

UNFORTUNATELY, THE months passed quickly, and their wedding day arrived without Owen and Lily stealing a minute of alone time. It would've been laughable except for the apprehension she felt.

Fate's already tipping the scales against us. Again.

Standing in the countess's suite in the Trent's London home, Lily sucked in a breath as Caraway tried to button the row of pearl buttons lining the front.

"I thought Mrs. Fleur was supposed to be the premier modiste in London. Because if these are the measurements she took, they are woefully wrong." Cara tugged the silky fabric together, careful to balance force and delicacy, as she tried again.

"I'm not sure..." Hazel said, eyeing Lily speculatively. "You do look a bit... fuller, dear. Perhaps a spat of nervous eating has led to an increase? I know you and Owen want everyone to believe everything's settled between the two of you, but neither of you are as good of actors as you'd like to think."

"It's not nervous eating. Besides, I've kept with my daily exertions around the lake, despite the nausea I've felt every morning." Lily snapped her fingers as another realization hit. "Which also should've helped me decrease. This doesn't make any sense."

"Nausea?" Cara asked, pausing her ministrations to step back and study Lily. Three pairs of curious gazes studied her, and she had the sneaking suspicion this is what it felt like to be one of her Papa's old research specimens.

"It's nothing. It goes away soon after appearing."

Another weighted silence bloomed before her eldest sister's eyes widened and a stern frown of disapproval tightened her mouth. "Lily Nicole Taylor. Please tell me you're not increasing... with a child?"

Iris covered a startled gasp, and disbelief ballooned in Lily's chest. "Of course not! I've had my monthlies—as sporadic as they are. But you know how I've always had light spotting."

"You can spot while pregnant, dear," Hazel informed them. Since becoming a school teacher, she'd begun inundating them with random facts. This, however, was not one Lily cared to hear.

"Have you had any other symptoms?" Iris asked.

"It was the night of the ball, wasn't it?" Caraway blurted at the same time. "You and Owen disappeared, then you left for the night. Goodness, Lily! That was almost four months ago! You're halfway through your pregnancy, and we're just now learning about this? Does Owen know?"

"How could he? I didn't know until this moment. If I'm to believe it's true, which I'm not entirely convinced." She couldn't be pregnant with Owen's baby—his heir.

Oh, god.

A wave of dizziness slammed into her, and she reached for the nearest object for stability, her flabbergasted sister. Caraway remained rooted to the floor, curling an arm around Lily while sweeping a curl off Lily's gleaming forehead, the heat in the room rising to an unbearable limit.

"Now, now. You'll be alright. We're here to aid you anyway we can, and the good news is you'll be the Countess of Trent by the end of the day. Some may question the birth's timetable, but most will overlook it considering your standing in Society."

"I don't care about Society's opinion." Lily gulped the glass of water Iris poured for her. "I can't be a mother. I'm not ready."

If I'll ever be.

Children had never featured prominently in Lily's future after Owen's departure. Spinsterhood reared its ugly head, along with the range of emotional upheaval she still contended with. She was too brash. Too mean to have a baby. To be a mother.

Cara sighed and turned pragmatic. "You'll be ready when it's time. Every woman feels this way at some point."

"How do you know?" Lily snapped, eyes heated before she caught a glimpse of her dark expression in the mirror. *A perfect example of how little control I have over myself.*

Pressing a slick palm to her stomach, she prayed her sisters were wrong. *You know they aren't.* Her symptoms added up to pregnancy.

Curse Owen!

How on earth had he managed to impregnate her so quickly? Their coupling had lasted mere seconds. She knew about eggs and fertilization through her father's science journals, but this seemed far-fetched.

Another one of life's cruel jokes.

Yes, that made sense. The most sensible conclusion to come from the past five minutes.

"I don't, but I prefer optimism over your pessimistic musings," Cara scolded before wrestling with the pearl buttons until they cinched over Lily's growing body. Thank goodness, the gown still fit. *Barely*. She didn't remember her breasts feeling quite so crushed under the bodice, the quality fabric chafing.

However, even if the dress fit more tightly than intended, at least it remained wearable. She couldn't imagine explaining to Lady Trent why the custom-made gown she'd bought no longer matched Lily's expanding measurements.

"It's best to be realistic," Lily retorted under her breath, but allowed the topic to dwindle away. Now wasn't the time to argue as her sisters escorted her downstairs to a waiting carriage that would carry them to St. George's.

They had a wedding ceremony to attend.

CHAPTER EIGHT

We're to be parents. Can you believe it? In truth, you're the only man I saw myself bearing children for, but reality is far more complicated than I expected.

"MY LORD, MIGHT I HAVE a word?" The Marquess of Linton approached Owen later in the afternoon as he prepared to notify Lily of their ability to finally leave. They'd dined and chatted for hours after their vows were spoken, and he knew it was wearing on her.

Scanning the bobbing heads before him for the sight of his newly minted wife, Owen nodded absent-mindedly to the older gentleman. "Certainly. What's this about?"

"I wanted to congratulate you on your nuptials. It was a lovely ceremony, and the bride looked quite beautiful. You're a lucky fellow." *Indeed.* The image of Lily walking down the aisle towards him, draped in cream lace and silk, would forever linger in his mind. "However, I couldn't help but notice one of her... sisters, is it? The pale blonde?"

If this man wished to express a romantic interest in Iris, he was wasting his time. The remaining unwed Taylor sisters wouldn't have to marry for anything but love after the dowries and trusts he'd set up for them. And while Iris was sweet and amenable to everyone, he doubted her first choice of husband would be a man old enough to be her father.

"Miss Iris. What about her?"

"She bears a striking resemblance to my late sister Agatha—similar coloring in the hair and eyes—and it occurred to me that there might have been consequences from an ill-fated affair years ago. If you understand my meaning..." The marquess raised a steel gray eyebrow while Owen struggled to comprehend the enormity of what the man was implying. In the middle of a damned wedding reception, no less!

Drawing him to the side of the room for more privacy, Owen asked, "Are you suggesting Miss Iris is your daughter? A bastard child?"

"I wouldn't have put it so harshly, but yes. Her mother is Miss Martha Kent, correct?"

He had to give the man credit with the naming of Iris's true mother. Most people in Shoreham had forgotten the abrupt appearance of another baby at the Taylor home only a few short months after Mrs. Taylor birthed Caraway. Though technically a cousin, she'd been raised as a sister since infancy, and the villagers accepted it as truth after so many years.

The fact that Linton knew of Iris's true origins meant there may be some validity to his claim. "She is. Or was, rather. She passed two years after abandoning her baby with her sister, Mrs. Taylor. If you believe you're her father, what do you plan to do about it? Acknowledge her in front of Society?"

The marquess didn't possess a sterling reputation as is, so a bastard child emerging from his past wouldn't be remarkable. However, Owen didn't like the idea of Iris being exposed to vicious gossip.

AN EARL LIKE ANY OTHER

"She's a marquess's daughter! The blood running in her veins matches my own." Puffing out his chest, the man resembled a bloated peacock—his overblown facsimile of fatherly concern put Owen on edge. "I'd like to get to know my daughter, since I was robbed of the chance. Her mother deserted me with no warning."

Which fit the brief description Lily had given him of her aunt when they were younger.

"I'll need to speak with the family and Miss Iris about such a meeting. She's lived over two decades without you; I'm not sure how good it'd be for you to crop up in her life now."

Understatement of the century. The family had just dodged the bullet of Mr. Laramie. Now, they may have Iris's biological father to contend with?

Life with the Garden Girls guaranteed to never be boring.

Finally, spotting his wife in the crowd, he cut Linton's forceful defense off with a head shake. "No more. You've said your piece, and I'll consider what you're asking. For now, that is all I can give you." Without another word, Owen cut through groups of guests congratulating him on his nuptials before cosying up behind Lily, who kept her gaze fixed on a discussion between Caraway and Lord Brandon.

"You need more male friends."

They watched as Caraway laughed at something Brandon said, her body inching closer to his. He'd suspected Cara's crush when they were younger, but he'd hoped she would have grown out of it by now. Unfortunately, time and distance seemed to make her heart grow fonder as she blushed at another quip by his friend.

"You and your sisters were... are the closest friends I have," he admitted. "I got along fine with the boys at school, but we never formed a kinship like I did with your family. Besides, you little hoydens stole any energy I might have had left for other friendships."

"Hoydens!" She smacked his arm in mock effrontery before turning back to the tableau before them.

"Don't pretend the moniker doesn't fit."

"Perhaps, though I'm sure Cara's never been described that way in her life. Either way, you're a grown man now who needs peers to confide in, other than Brandon. Cara's too taken with him, and I get the impression that he just enjoys attention from wherever he can get it."

She wasn't wrong. And he disliked his sister-in-law being hurt in the process.

"What about Jonathan, Hazel's husband?"

"I'm still reserving judgment on him." Their gazes switched to the couple on the other side of the room—a former criminal turned legitimate businessman and his cheerful wife.

"They've been married nigh on eight months without issue. I think it's high time you gave the man a chance."

"Perhaps, but as a former rookery rogue, I find it hard to believe a tiger could so easily change its stripes." An unbecoming comparison to his wife came to mind. Had she changed her stripes? Could she be trusted again?

"Doesn't the saying mention something about spots instead of stripes?" Lily smirked, a teasing sparkle in her hazel eyes, and he prayed she could be.

"Focus, darling. Either way, I'm not ready to confide my deeply personal secrets to Mr. Jonathan Travers."

"Oh no, you should only share those with me. But at least if you spent more time with Jonathan, Brandon wouldn't be around so much. I hate seeing Cara so obviously smitten with someone unworthy of her."

Sighing in resignation, he agreed. "I know. I've tried hinting that he's not the man for her, but she ignores the subtle warnings. And of course, I can't share the truly sordid parts of Brandon since she's a lady."

Lily perked up at the chance to learn more about Brandon's flaws. "Tell me, and I'll tell her. I have no qualms about sharing such information."

"Incorrigible minx."

"Stick in the mud."

"Since when is caring about propriety and protecting your sister's sensibilities considered being a stick in the mud?" Turning away from the pair, Owen's brow raised in question.

"Since always, dear. Stop worrying about Cara's sensibilities." Taking a sip of the champagne in her hand, she continued, "They're not delicate in the least, and you'd be saving her from heartache."

"Which you're the expert on." The unconscious jab hit its mark as a wounded expression chased the playful expression from Lily's face. "I'm sorry; I don't know why I said that."

"It was an accurate assessment, however. I hardly know proper protocol when it comes to saving one from relational heartache. And I doubt Cara would appreciate my efforts. Or yours, for that matter." Studying the floating bubbles in her glass, she reverted back to their previous conversation. "Which brings me back to the original point. You need more male friends."

"I'll add it to my ever-growing list of responsibilities. Happy?"

"Moderately."

"Ah, we're progressing nicely then, because earlier I could've sworn you were hovering around a *barely*. Keep this up, and we might reach emotions of joy before the evening is done." He winked before avoiding the closed fan that slipped off her wrist to fly towards him after her imitation of hitting him over the head went awry.

The piece landed at his mother's feet while surrounding guests tittered at the outburst. "My, you two are in high spirits. Should I ask what has elicited such a reaction from our dear countess? Wedding revels?"

"She thinks I need more friends."

"Touchy topic, I see." His mother smiled before picking up the discarded fan. "Though, I agree with her. It would be nice to see you relaxing with your peers rather than hiding away in your study. Something that will surely change with Lily's permanent presence."

Groaning, Owen warned. "Don't you start, too. I'm going to make the rounds one more time before we say our goodbyes. Care to join me, wife?"

Lily startled at the title but nodded, her elaborate coiffure bouncing in time with the movement. He couldn't wait to see the thick strands loose and spread on his bed.

Don't get too excited. You've no idea how tonight will proceed.

But a man could hope.

Spying Cara and Iris alone, no Brandon in sight, Owen took advantage and guided them towards the remaining unattached Taylor sisters.

"Are you ladies enjoying yourselves?" he asked as they hugged him and Lily.

"Very much. Your mother has done a wonderful job of organizing and the church looked as if it'd been plucked from the pages of a fairytale," Iris gushed, ever the romantic. The discussion with Linton threatened to burst forth, but another disclosure needed to be spoken first.

"I will let her know of your approval." Clearing his throat, his grasp tightened on Lily. "I want the both of you to know you'll always be taken care of—whether you marry or not. Dowries and trusts have been set up in your names, so you needn't worry about money any longer."

Cara and Iris stared, mouths agape. Spluttering, the elder sister responded first. "You can't be serious. This is too generous! We have Papa's savings left, which will last for the foreseeable future now that you've dealt with Mr. Laramie. You've done enough."

He knew Cara would present the most challenge, be the most adamant against him providing the Garden Girls with financial aid. She was the most independent sister, rivaling Lily for the title, though she hid the streak well under propriety and calm.

Surprisingly, his wife voiced no objection. Just surveyed him beneath furrowed brows, an unreadable expression masking her face.

"You are too kind, Owen." Iris smiled and glided forward to wrap him in another hug. Guilt shaded the moment as he recalled his conversation with her possible biological father, but now wasn't the time to bring it up.

"Yes, too kind," Lily murmured at his side. It lacked any snideness, though, and he wondered what was going through her mind.

"It's the least I can do for my family, which you've always been, even if today's when it became official." He'd failed his duty to them during his extended leave, allowing Laramie to barge in with ultimatums, but the corrected course lay before him now.

Owen would ensure his sisters-in-law's well-being while attempting to achieve happiness with his wife.

A quest slated to begin that very night.

CHAPTER NINE

Your countess yearns for you. And fears you. Or rather, the emotions I feel whenever you're near. I'm sorry I'm so much trouble.

THE LUXURIOUS BED PILED with fluffy pillows called Lily's name. After a day full of socializing and revelations—Owen's generosity to her sisters still stunned her—she found herself preparing for her first night as a wife—as a countess.

There wouldn't be a traditional wedding night between them, of course, but Lily did need to tell Owen of her suspicions that she might be pregnant.

How would he receive the news? Joyfully? Fiercely? Would he storm out of her suite?

"Will there be anything else, my lady?" The young maid assigned to assist Lily stopped at the door with an expectant look.

"No, thank you, Hildy. That will be all." She wasn't used to requiring someone's help dressing or undressing, someone whose sole purpose was to see to her needs, and it didn't feel right. Lily had taken care of herself for years. Just because a title preceded her name now didn't mean she'd suddenly developed an aversion to such things.

A knock at the door connecting her suite to Owen's punctured the quiet interlude, and she turned expectantly for his entrance. Black silk draped his broad shoulders, falling to bare feet, as he strode inside wearing nothing but a robe.

Oh, my.

He was a virile man—tall, lean, and golden but for the auburn crowning his head.

"Good evening, Lily-pad. Have you decided how we're to proceed tonight?" The drawl of his old nickname for her sent a shiver down her spine as he pinned her with an indolent stare.

Picking up an enamel-crusted hairbrush from the vanity, she faced the mirror and drew the bristles through her long hair, evincing the same nonchalant attitude. "Not quite. You see, I have news of my own to impart." Inhaling through her nose, Lily met his admiring gaze in the mirror. "It appears that I am, indeed, pregnant with your child. The question now, my lord, is how do you wish to proceed?"

Like a fish out of water, Owen's mouth opened and closed in shock, searching for words that would not come. She almost felt guilty for battering him over the head with their impending parenthood, especially since she'd explained how she wasn't pregnant after her first supposed monthly.

"But you said..." He glanced towards her stomach, hidden behind the silken folds of her wrapper. "You said you weren't with child, but now you are? How is this possible?"

Oh, dear lord.

She hadn't considered the awkwardness of explaining her womanly cycle. Such things weren't discussed with men. They were barely mentioned among women. Flushing to the roots of her hair, Lily relayed the irregular nature of her cycles and Hazel's tidbit about bleeding while pregnant. Through stutters and hard swallows, Lily managed to spit out a semi-coherent explanation, and throughout it all, the air seemed to leave Owen, breath by breath, until he sat deflated in an armchair by the fireplace.

"A babe is on the way. We're having a child."

"Of course, it hasn't been confirmed by a doctor. Only my persistent symptoms. But it seems likely that yes, we're expecting."

She continued her nightly routine as he digested the information. To be fair, it had taken her the majority of the day to come to terms with it. Though not elated over these unexpected circumstances, she accepted them.

As she accepted every bad turn life threw in her path.

It's your child, not a bad turn, she chided inwardly. But she couldn't help the negative weight bearing down on her chest from the knowledge of her imminent motherhood.

"If it's all the same to you, it might be best if we forgo our conjugal rights tonight." Owen swiped a hand through his hair, causing a few strands to stick up in the back.

"Agreed. Too much remains unsettled for us to jump into bed together, despite our marriage status." Her pesky desires could simmer down in the meantime as Lily eyed the broad chest peeking through the vee of Owen's robe.

We're being logical adults, no more reckless behavior! We see where that's led.

"Oh, we'll be sharing a bed." A smug twinkle entered his gaze. "I'd like to start as I intend to continue, which is sleeping in the same room as my wife."

Her mouth opened for a rebuttal, but he raised a hand in caution. "Sleeping only. For now."

"Can you handle such an arrangement?" Unwillingly, Lily's perusal dropped to the bulge beneath his robe, not fully erect from her observation, but still interested.

"That, my dear, remains to be seen. But I'm willing to try. Are you?" He dared to wink at her, plucking the blankets back from their tucked in positions before climbing into *her* bed. "Can I trust you to keep your hands to yourself?"

"Naturally. I am a lady, after all."

"Another freshly-acquired label, if memory serves."

Slipping the silk wrapper off her shoulders, she reveled in Owen's abrupt silence at her dishabille. Her nightgown wasn't particularly scandalous, a white cotton gown that brushed the carpet at her feet. Even her arms were covered.

But his rapt attention blanketed her in warmth.

And suddenly, the night became a game of wills—one she intended to win.

Snuggling into her pillow beside him, Lily released an exaggerated yawn, stretching her arms overhead and causing her breasts to stretch the thin fabric tightly, revealing the budded nipples. "A lady, a wife, a countess. Take your pick, husband, but while you're debating, I believe it's time I rested. Do stick to your side of the bed, hmm?"

With a twitch of her backside, she rolled over, hiding an impish grin of delight.

A SPLASH OF WATER RAINED over her shoulders, the gleaming droplets shining like diamonds in the sun. Owen dipped beneath the waterline before she could retaliate, and soon she found herself dragged under, caught in his grasp.

She shouldn't be here.

The unwelcome thought wavered into conscience.

Bursting from the lake with a gasp for oxygen, Lily slapped Owen's bare chest as he laughed and towed her closer, his heat seeping through their wet clothes.

"Are you trying to drown me?"

"Would I save you if I were?" His arms pressed her deeper into him, hot arousal tempting her to rub against the thick cock wedged between them.

"Trying to seduce me, then? Get me within your devious clutches?" Her hands flexed on his shoulders as she rolled her hips into his, legs wrapping around a lean waist.

"Now, you've the right of it," he admitted before dipping his head and capturing her lips with his.

A low moan of pleasure rippled through her, breaking the barrier between dream and reality. *What?* Lashes slowly blinking open, Lily oriented herself in the unfamiliar setting.

This isn't the lake.

And she wasn't a girl of eighteen.

But that is Owen's hard erection nudging my thigh!

Snapping to full awareness, comprehension worked its way into her fuzzy brain. Owen lay beneath her. Some time in the night, she'd accosted him in her sleep, climbing over his large body to blanket it from head to toe.

Please, don't wake. Please, don't wake.

The humiliation of being caught by him in such a compromising position would be too much after her taunting the night before. Easing her arm and leg to the mattress, Lily gingerly scooted away from Owen, a tiny breath of relief escaping.

Rays of sunshine crisscrossed the floor, and the smells of breakfast wafted up from the kitchen. She'd dress quickly and eat before he ever awakened, then she'd put this lapse behind her. Plan set, Lily made haste, tugging on an old day dress that buttoned up the front and left before Hildy could knock to offer help.

Bumping into the maid on her way downstairs, Lily informed her to let the earl sleep, a flush of scarlet blossoming at the woman's knowing stare, before continuing her journey below.

Goodness. What a morning!

Seeking respite after an amiable breakfast with the dowager countess—another knowing smirk appearing at the absence of her tired son—Lily excused herself for a walk in the gardens. She wished she'd thought to wear her normal attire of breeches and shirt for more taxing exercise, but it was unclear how she should act as countess now.

While rules didn't particularly matter to her, she didn't relish the idea of embarrassing Owen or his mother by continuing her peculiar habits.

A subdued meow sounded from the bushes to the right as Lily soaked in the warm sunshine, hoping its cheerful light might drive out the unsettling emotions plaguing her at the moment. Following the pitiful whine, Lily again lamented the lack of trousers as she awkwardly knelt in her skirts to see a calico cat huddled behind a shrubbery root, paw stuck between two branches.

"Well, hello, little one." Her voice soothed in the wake of the feline's fear-filled eyes. "You've gotten yourself into a bit of a pickle, haven't you? Don't worry. I'll free you... somehow."

Leaning forward, Lily reached through the branches—rough bark scraping her skin—to free the stuck paw. She assumed the cat would immediately scamper away, but instead it surprised her by inching closer to the edge of her spread skirt, peeking through the dense bottom branches of the bush. "My, you're a brave one, aren't you?" An answering meow elicited an amused grin from her.

Tentative paws patted the hem of her dress, nails clinging to the fabric before flexing to release it. It'd been years since she'd had a pet. Not since their old dog Boris died.

A companion might be just what she needed in this new environment.

Coming to a similar conclusion, the feline traipsed forward to knead her paws into Lily's leg. "Careful, shield those claws, if you please." Contented purring accompanied the gentle kneading, and she noticed an obvious bulge around the cat's stomach.

"Why, you're expecting kittens!"

A deeper purr rumbled in the air. "We're both to be mothers, then, hmm?" Lily's head tilted towards the sky, a bemused smile gracing her cheeks. For once, fate did one thing right—sending her the perfect kindred spirit to share her trials with.

CHAPTER TEN

The image of you and Zinnia never crossed my mind as particularly stimulating, yet discovering the two of you playing in your study while I watched from the hall... Well, let's just say if you and a feline does something to my heart, I fear what will happen when I see you with our child.

A TIED SCROLL RESTED on Owen's desk in the study, along with the rest of the day's post. *Odd.* Who sent scrolls these days?

Untying the black ribbon, he skimmed the short sentence scrawled in ink: *You're a disgrace to your father marrying that girl.*

Anger, swift and lethal, punched him in the gut as he crumpled the sheet in his fist. Who would dare to send such a revolting reprimand? Especially after his wedding!

And to mention his father...

"There you are, my lord." The butler entered quietly. "I see you've found the incoming post from today, quite a stack. Would you like me to send for Mr. Foreman to aid you?"

"No, thank you. But I would like to know if anything came with this particular letter?" He smoothed out the crinkled parchment, holding it aloft for the man to see. "I'm curious about its author."

Marvin squinted at the words, eyes widening at the message, before shaking his head vigorously. "No, my lord! If I had known such vitriol blackened the note, I would've never let it cross the threshold!"

Jaw tightening, Owen trusted the man's righteous outrage and waved him away. "If another arrives, see if you can discern who's sending them before giving it to me. Say nothing of this to anyone, especially her ladyship."

He didn't need Lily hearing about someone writing ominous letters about their marriage. They were already on shaky ground with their own problems; no need to add an outsider's.

Slumping into his desk chair, Owen recalled Lily's bombshell—a baby was on the way. Their brief tryst had resulted in something, after all, and he wondered what she would have done if Laramie hadn't forced the issue of their marriage.

Would she have even told him about the child?

They most certainly would not have married so easily, since he would've had to overcome Lily's reservations.

The surprising meow of an animal drifted into the room, followed by his wife and a colorful fur ball clinging to her chest. Distracted from thoughts that would surely lead him down a path of frustration, he scrambled to his feet and asked, "What is that?"

"A cat, obviously." Lily rolled her eyes heavenward and stepped closer to allow him to study the bundle of matted fur at its back. "This is Zinnia. I found her in the bushes in one of the gardens. Her poor paw was stuck, and I saved her. Will this be an issue?" A mutinous line formed on her mouth, challenging him to refuse her this feline friend.

Owen ran a hand over a patch of white fur and sighed. "Of course not, but make sure you have one of the maids clean it. I don't want you catching anything if it has fleas, especially in your condition."

"I'm pregnant, Owen, not incapable of bathing an animal or taking care of myself."

"I know, but indulge me. We have servants for a reason."

"You have servants. Before yesterday, I tended to my own needs like most people."

"What's mine is yours, Lily-pad. Already forgetting those vows we took? Has it even been twenty-four hours?" he teased, his fingers accidentally tangling with hers in the midst of their petting. Her hand bounced away, but not before he caught the slightest caress of a finger over his skin.

When he'd awakened alone that morning, a wave of disgruntlement had cascaded through him. He'd wanted to see her lithe form sleeping beside his, not empty blankets like every day prior.

"Trust me, I remember, but it's going to take time before I become accustomed to having aid whenever I call for it." Switching back to Zinnia, Lily added, "She's pregnant, too, you know? Seems fairly far along based on the swell of her tummy, though I'm not exactly a veterinarian."

"So, we'll have kittens before a baby. Fitting practice?" Their eyes met over Zinnia, and the ghost of a smile flashed before disappearing.

"Everyone adores kittens. I'm sure they'll be taken off our hands before any practice starts. But I don't mind. Zinnia's the real keeper—my very own lap cat."

"I wouldn't mind having my very own lap wife." He felt silly the moment the words left his mouth, but he pressed on, sliding an arm around Lily's waist and gently urging her down to sit on his thighs as he returned to his seat. The supple weight of her bottom rubbing against his groin wrested a pained groan to well up as his cock hardened at the contact.

"Owen!" she hissed, wiggling in his hold. Zinnia disliked the sudden movement and hopped onto his desk, disrupting the stacks of work previously placed in an orderly fashion. He couldn't give a damn. "What do you think you're doing? Someone could see us... Your mother could discover us!" An adorable gasp trembled on her lips as her squirming persisted.

"Then they'll all be scandalized and secretly glad to see the earl and his countess getting along so well."

"But are we? Everything's happened so fast in such a short time span. We've hardly had time to adjust to one another... as we are now and not... before." *Before.* When youthful fantasies dominated their lives rather than the less-fantastical reality they found themselves in now.

He supposed the moment had come to clarify what happened seven years ago. To finally learn why she'd so cruelly broken his heart.

"Lily, why—"

"Apologies, sir, but there's been a mishap at the Henley construction site. A beam slipped its holding and landed on Garrett Henley. The men are trying to excavate him, but they could use more help." A harried-looking man ran a tattered rag over his ruddy face as Marvin stood apologetically behind him.

Dammit. Just when Lily and he were making progress, a wrench was thrown into things.

"Notify Dr. Pearson, if he hasn't been already, and round up any spare footmen along with saddling my horse, Marvin. I shall ride out immediately." Helping Lily to her feet, he appreciated the glow of concern emanating from her, resting a palm on her cheek before leaving.

A sturdier barn was being built at the Henleys, one better-suited to housing their livestock. He hated that their eldest son was now injured from the project.

I'll help however I can. It's what Father would do.

Owen headed upstairs to change into more suitable attire for manual labor before jogging outside to where his gelding, River, waited in the hands of a young stable boy. The Henleys were located on the eastern portion of his lands, and he took off at a gallop, the weight of his responsibilities chasing him across fields of green.

Husband.

Son.

Earl.

Soon-to-be-father.

Caretaker of his tenants.

The list grew longer and longer, and he wondered if his seven-year desertion wasn't catching up to him. If this wasn't punishment for being away for so long.

For abandoning his mother after the death of her beloved husband.

For choosing Lily against his father's well-meaning advice.

CHAPTER ELEVEN

We were interrupted today. It was probably for the best, but know I dreamed of our interlude last night, and this time Marvin didn't bother us in the least.

"IT SHALL BE OUR FIRST event as a married couple. We can't not attend!" Owen tossed the invitation to the table in front of Lily and stomped to the other side of the room, his raised voice exacerbating the onset of the migraine she feared was coming.

After a week of amiable conversations and tiptoeing around each other—using his mother and Brandon, who remained a guest, as buffers—it seemed the unspoken peace was at an end. A part of her brightened, since Owen had been the perfect gentleman for days now. Solicitous and gentle, ensuring anything she needed—including a doctor to confirm her state of pregnancy. The number of times she'd cried randomly at an act of kindness was beginning to wear on her nerves.

So, this man? The upset and belligerent Owen? She could handle him without an explosion of tears.

Hopefully.

"There will be another ball or musical or some other silly event soon enough that will be our first together. Give my regrets for this one." Neighboring nobles had discovered that the Earl and Countess of Trent had not booked a honeymoon, instead opting to stay in Hampshire, which meant a flood of invitations overflowed their post. One such invite taunted her from its thrown position.

She surreptitiously tilted her head down to avoid the direct light piercing through the window across from her place on the settee. The bright beacon ushered in the first wave of pulsating pain at her temples, and her lashes fluttered closed for a brief reprieve.

"The Duke of Lansing was my father's oldest friend. I will not disrespect him by showing up sans my wife after we already agreed to go. Especially when there's no valid reason for your refusal to attend."

Oh, she had a reason, but she loathed sharing the weakness with him.

"Why must our first outing be one so highly sought after? Everyone will stare. Curious about the country upstart the Earl of Trent chained himself to. I'd rather not feel like a bug under a microscope straight out of the gate." A minute shudder wracked her body as another pointed spear of pain buried itself in her head. "Let's ease into things with a smaller, more intimate affair."

"That would have been my preference," Owen relented. "However, we said we'd attend this one. His Grace is expecting us." Raking a hand through his hair, he marched back to stand before Lily and she forced her gaze up to meet his, praying he'd mistake the tightness in her mouth, the cloudiness glazing her eyes, for frustration rather than illness.

"Let's compromise. We'll attend the ball for the minimum amount of time we can get away with, and you get to choose the next invitation we accept. Deal?"

It was fair. She knew it was fair. But she knew her migraine would not subside by that evening.

She could not go.

"No."

"For the love of..." The epithet ended quietly, under his breath, confusion and anger warring for dominance in his countenance. And she had no doubt another tirade was imminent, except a subtle knock heralded a visitor before Marvin interrupted with a package for Owen.

Taking advantage of the distraction, Lily stood, bracing a hand on the back of the settee for support as her knees threatened to buckle. "Excuse me, I'll leave you to your business." Hasty footsteps led to her bedroom, where Hildy gathered her garments for washing.

"My lady." The girl dipped into a quick curtsy. Her brows raised as she took in Lily's pale appearance. "Are you unwell? Shall I fetch a doctor?"

"That won't be necessary. All I need is solitude. Please close the drapes and bring a warm bowl of water with a rag. My head is aching, and those two things are the most important items of aid." Throbbing agony formed behind her right eye. Her argument with Owen, along with the pregnancy, was taking its toll.

"Yes, my lady." Quick as a fox, Hildy completed her tasks before helping Lily undress to her chemise and carefully closing the door to leave her ladyship in peace.

Crawling into the bed with a groan, she rolled to her back and stared up at the canopied top, fighting a wave of tears. "You'll be fine. This will pass," she whispered to herself in encouragement. Lily wrung out the clean rag, water dripping from her hands to the bowl, then placed the folded piece of cloth over her eyes. A sigh of relief expelled from her chest as heat seeped into her skin, attempting to soothe the pain.

She hated these episodes.

All her life she'd been fit as a fiddle, never prone to illness. Yet, everything had changed as the dominoes of her life steadily fell into ruin. From the scandal with Asa and Owen to her parents' deaths, the stress and bitterness combined into a malady of migraines she couldn't shake no matter how hard she tried. Her sisters had learned to avoid her for the day when one came on.

Errant tears escaped beneath the rag.

Was pain—physical and emotional—to rule her days now?

A plaintive meow preceded the arrival of Zinnia, her warm body slinking along Lily's as she crept up the mattress to curl into the curve of her bent legs. Smoothing a hand over her fur, Lily appreciated the company. Low purrs vibrated between them, loosening the self-pity she'd been wallowing in, and filling her with calm instead.

Wordless gratitude etched the fingers tracing the small bones lining Zinnia's back. "You're a sweet girl, aren't you?"

This was what she needed: a companion who asked for little from her but provided comfort in return. Owen flashed through her mind, and she couldn't resist giving into her weakness—fantasizing about his warm strength comforting her, too.

That way lies trouble.

Somehow, she'd avoided waking in his arms again after that first unexpected morning. Though, the playful flirting he'd initiated later on plagued her dreams.

Forcing her thoughts in another direction, an image of the lake appeared—calm and serene. Gentle waves lapped the shores and carried her away from her troubles as she floated in the rippling water.

"Don't think you can avoid the party by pretending to be ill. I'm not falling for your ruse, so you can quit being dramatic." Her husband's booming voice and the slamming of the door broke the moment, causing her to flinch at the loud noises.

"Not now, Owen." She pushed the words out in a weak plea for peace.

"We're going to have this out. I've never known you to be one to avoid a confrontation and certainly not by acting frail. Iris commented on migraines at my mother's ball, but I never..." His voice faltered, and she could imagine the racing thoughts forming behind those gray eyes. The Lily of seven years ago—the Lily he knew—would've scoffed at the notion of being laid low by illness, especially one as seemingly innocuous as a headache.

But this was no ordinary headache. And her body had changed in the intervening years, not the least of which with her more recent condition of pregnancy.

With a sigh, she dragged the damp rag off her face and peeked at Owen from slitted eyes. "This..." She paused as a particularly vehement crash of nausea hit her. Breathing deeply through her nose, a continuous prayer began in her mind as she concentrated on not casting up her accounts.

Trying again, she whispered, "This isn't me pretending—" Another pang roiled in her stomach, urging her to swallow hard, the sickly bile burning in her throat; she'd done enough vomiting to last her a lifetime due to the baby. This migraine wasn't going to get the best of her, too, especially not in front of an unsympathetic Owen.

The man in question stepped closer. His gaze tracked around the room, noting the closed curtains, the bowl of cooling water, and Zinnia, before returning to study her prone form. Finally, it seemed her weakened condition broke through his frustration. Brow wrinkled in concern, his haughty demeanor abated.

"What's wrong? Is it the baby?"

"The baby's fine. It's just a migraine."

The bed dipped with added weight as he bent over her. Moaning, she tried to avoid the gentle touch of his fingertips on her cheek. "No, I don't want you near me."

He ignored the faint plea as he began massaging her temples. The tender touch brought more tears to the forefront.

Oh, god, not more.

"I always cry when you're like this. Why are you kind to me?" she asked, bewildered by the sudden change in his demeanor.

"I wasn't kind earlier when I barged in like a boorish oaf."

"But I deserved that. I didn't explain why I couldn't go."

AN EARL LIKE ANY OTHER

"You may frustrate me, Lily-pad. There's no denying it. But ultimately, your welfare is my priority. No matter how upset I am, I don't want you suffering, and I'll try to alleviate whatever I can." The soothing strokes along her head continued. "We'll send our regrets to Lansing. He'll understand."

Respite curled through her at his sweet words—if only words were enough to heal her completely.

Owen disappeared for a moment, murmuring in the hall drifting into the room. *I suppose those are our regrets being posted*, she mused, before Owen returned to his position behind her. Relaxing under his touch, she allowed herself to accept Owen's care as he extended the massage down to her neck and shoulders before tracing a path back towards her temple.

"There's nothing that can help," she admitted reluctantly, recalling the many powders and teas she'd tried to cure the affliction. "I've had enough of these to know the only way past it is to let it run its course." His firm chest provided a warm support for her back, and the muscles along her spine and shoulders loosened, releasing some of their pent-up tension. "All I really need is the quiet and darkness."

"Okay," he whispered, and they lay together until the light filtering through the edges of the drapes dimmed and black shadows settled over the room.

WHEN DAWN DRIFTED OVER the horizon, Lily opened her eyes to see golden light inching across the Aubusson carpet. A breath of relief left her as she woke free of pain—the hours of sleep with Owen allowing it to finally pass. His arms remained around her in a protective hold, and Lily relished the sense of security it provided—even if she knew it couldn't last.

Their problems weren't resolved, despite this détente.

Enjoy the moment, for once. It doesn't always have to be doom and gloom.

Deciding to heed the advice, she shimmied further into his body and hugged his arm closer. Owen's chest pressed into her back as a puff of air ruffled the tiny hairs at her nape before he nuzzled closer. "How are you feeling?" His low whisper brushed over her skin like the lightest feathers drifting from a nest.

"Better. The hammering ache is gone."

"I'm glad. How long have you been dealing with this? I've never known you to be sick in all the years of our acquaintance."

Because her life had been different then.

"You won't like the answer. They started after our... falling out."

"How politely stated." She gave him credit for a tone devoid of ire.

"And after the accident claimed our parents' lives and almost Hazel's, they became increasingly frequent. I suppose my body had reached its limit of hardship." And now she was married with a child on the way—what possible trouble would that add to her strained mind?

Mirroring her thoughts, Owen spoke. "And now we're here together and expecting a child. I'm guessing our argument caused this flare-up?"

"It's never based on an isolated event," she explained, turning to face him. "But I'm sure it didn't help."

A sliver of remorse crept forward in his expression. At least now, their argument was moot. They'd missed the ball last night while sleeping her migraine away.

Leaning forward, he brushed a tender kiss across her forehead. "I'm sorry. I should've paid better attention to you instead of flying off the handle."

"I forgive you." *For everything.*

Owen treated her well, despite her actions against him. It was time for her to forgive the way he reacted to Asa's story and accept her part in it—even if it had been grossly exaggerated. An exaggeration that only would have occurred because she orchestrated the brief kiss with Asa in the first place.

At eighteen, she'd made a stupid mistake.

At twenty, he'd done the same.

It wasn't right to hold the consequences of her actions against him any longer.

Especially when he'd been so kind to her and her family. Paying off Laramie. Creating trusts and dowries for Iris and Caraway. Assuring her good health with visits from Dr. Pearson, and even sticking with her through her migraine.

Yes, it was time to forgive and move on as best they could.

A tentative knock came from the door before Hildy inched inside. "Good morning, my lord, my lady. Will you still be attending the village fair today?"

She'd forgotten entirely about it. One of her favorite times in Shoreham.

"I'm not sure..." Owen peered at her, studying the growing anticipation lighting her eyes. "Will we?"

"Yes, I wouldn't miss it for the world."

Thank goodness, her migraine occurred yesterday! Another small favor from fate.

CHAPTER TWELVE

You're too good for me, my love. Too kind. Too gentle. I'm undeserving.

IT'S FUNNY HOW MUCH life can change in a short period of time.

One could be gallivanting around Europe, pining for the lost love of his youth when, in a flash, one finds himself walking a dusty road with that very same love.

Owen glanced over at his wife as they strolled towards the village for the annual August fete, deciding the weather too congenial to ride cooped up in the carriage. He appreciated the exercise and the opportunity to have Lily completely to himself on the deserted path. The knowledge of her migraines shook him to the core. To see her brought so low fortified the wall of protection he wanted to give her, despite their rocky past.

Meekness had never been a part of his countess, yet it coated every word when she'd explained her condition to him.

Frankly, it didn't sit well.

Lily was fiery. She was stubborn and strong.

She did not fall victim to maladies.

That was the old Lily.

Dust tickling his nose, Owen sneezed and gratefully took the handkerchief Lily offered. "Thank you. Sometimes, I wonder if I've been so long away from England that my body's forgotten how to adjust to her nature as allergies abound."

"You have been rather sneezy and puffy lately," she agreed, a teasing lilt to her voice.

Affronted by the description, he shook his head vehemently. "I have never been puffy in my life. An earl is always dignified in disposition, even one afflicted with allergies."

"If you say so, my lord." She shrugged one elegant shoulder. Smiles played upon their mouths at the slight banter, until their wooden crossing came into view.

Shoreham Bridge.

The location of her parents' incident.

"Do you think of them often?" A picture of Owen's father presented itself in his mind as he considered their mutual loss. *At least I still have Mama.*

"Every day. You? With your father?"

"The same. Especially while handling estate affairs. He's a lot to live up to."

"Yes, he was a good man, though you are, too." The compliment didn't sound as difficult as he imagined it might be for her to announce. "You've always been intelligent and inventive. I'm sure whatever issues arise, you are more than capable of dealing with them."

Pride swelled in his chest at her adamant faith. He knew he was able, yet his mind absorbed it differently hearing the declaration from Lily. Her confidence in his abilities elicited a boyish need to preen and prove she was right to put such stock in him.

"Careful, you almost sounded wifely there."

An unladylike snort erupted at the accusation. "Oh, dear, I must be more careful…" Her amusement carried them across the bridge without falter, though Lily's hand strayed to the sturdy posts lining the rail more than once. "I envied your escape, you know."

"My escape?"

Red suffused her skin, a blush rather than a burn from the sun, underneath her bonnet. "Your great tour of the Continent. While precipitated by our falling out, it coincided with your father's sudden death as well." She chanced a peek up at him, and he felt the perusal of her gaze. "You have no idea how many times I wished I could leave this place after Mama and Papa died. When Hazel actually did leave, a certain jealousy took root then, too."

"I always thought I made the cowardly choice. Deserting Mama. Running from you. Seven years of running."

"If you're a coward, then so am I," she admitted. "Because I would've made the same choice."

"We always did share similarities."

"But our differences are glaring." *Perhaps not as much as they once were*, he thought. To his recollection, their differences served as the perfectly cut edges meant to fit together like puzzle pieces, creating a larger picture of harmony than the smaller discords would let on.

"How do you feel about Hazel's departure now? She seems happy with her life in Manchester, married and all."

"I'm glad she's found what she was searching for. To be honest, I've always loved it here. It's my home. My escape would have always been limited to a short time. I could never stay away for long."

Yes, he understood the sentiment. Being away from Hampshire had left a county-sized hole in his chest. His beloved home, mother, and the girl next door. They'd followed him through every museum, salon, and brothel Brandon imposed upon him.

Once again, their natures were in accord.

"I can't help a certain amount of amusement, though, at the thought of you going on your energetic promenades in Hyde Park in London. Civilized society would be scandalized."

"Then it's a good thing they don't know about the rest of my scandalous past. Or else the poor matrons would tumble into paroxysms of despair."

Chuckling, he agreed.

Chirping birds and the occasional trill of a breeze shifting through reeds followed them. Summer was in full effect with blue skies, white clouds, and rolling green hills as far as the eye could see. Owen inhaled a deep whiff of the sweet summer-grass and hummed in pleasure. He loved this time of year when everything lay in full bloom and the sun's rays saturated every dark corner leftover from winter.

Echoing the sentiment, Lily tipped her head back to soak in the summer heat, heedless of getting burned. "It's the perfect day for a fair. The whole village will be in attendance, I wager."

"No doubt, you're correct. Prepare yourself for a multitude of my lords and my ladies." An adorable moue brought her bottom lip into a full pout, and the temptation to kiss the pretty pink overwhelmed him. Everything about her overwhelmed him these days.

He'd heard tales of pregnancy being an intolerable nuisance for husbands as their wives complained of various pains and grew rounder with each passing month. But Owen didn't know what the devil was wrong with those men because Lily flourished with her condition.

Skin glowing with health. Breasts fuller in preparation for their babe. Every single change he'd witnessed served to draw him like honey to the bee. He only wished he could view them completely without barriers, but knew Lily wasn't ready for such intimacies yet. So, he comforted himself with the glimpses of flesh readily available to his thirsty gaze and prayed this drought would promptly end as their short journey neared its end, the village of Shoreham coming into view.

COLORFUL FLAGS FLUTTERED along clothing lines strung between the shops as Lily and Owen entered the village. Fair attendees roamed the street with hands full of shopping parcels and delicious treats, a contagious air of excitement emanating from the thoroughfare.

"What shall it be first? Food or exhibits?" Owen gestured towards the stalls set up along the grassy knoll behind the butcher's shop where livestock and acrobats reigned.

Stomach grumbling in answer, Lily pointed to a crowded vendor selling flavored ices. "Food."

"More like flavored water, but as my lady commands." A gallant bow waved her forward, and they weaved through the energetic crowd, Owen keeping a protective arm around her waist as he parted the waves of people. The chivalrous gesture melting her reserve.

"Has it always been this crowded? It seems to have grown three times since I last attended."

"Each year, more vendors come to peddle their wares. I believe Shoreham now holds the title of largest fair in the county."

"We ought to capitalize on that somehow."

"Spoken like a true businessman."

"My father would be proud," Owen quipped. "After our depleted coffers, he never looked down on those who worked for their living again. Especially since his father-in-law owned an impressive business, enabling him to give my mother a large enough dowry to save our hides."

"I suppose it's difficult to argue superiority of blood and laziness when all it landed you was trouble. I'm glad your father saw the error of his ways," she said as they moved to the end of a line for ices, slowly making their way towards the front.

Raised voices from the stall next door caught Lily's attention.

"I demand a refund!"

"But sir, three-quarters of the bag is gone. If you'd returned after first trying—"

"Are you calling me a liar?" A tall mustached man pointed his walking stick at the poor vendor with malice. "I am Sir Reginald Cook, and you shall treat me with respect!" Tossing a clearly opened and eaten bag of sweets to the counter, Sir Cook continued indignantly, "Return my money or else I shall accuse you of theft—of taking advantage of your customers."

"I recognize that look in your eyes. This is none of your concern," Owen warned by her ear, wrenching her from the perusal of the altercation.

"We can't allow that odious man to cheat them. He devoured those sweets and now wants to claim he didn't care for them? Wants his money back? That's what I call theft!"

"Lily-pad…"

But she was already exiting the line to confront this Sir Cook. "Excuse me, perhaps I could be of assistance. It is unfair of you to expect recompense after using this seller's product. If you had an issue with your order, the proper time to address it would've been immediately after you'd opened the bag. However, you chose to eat the majority of licorice anyway." Lily took a breath, marching closer to the stunned man. "Are you ill? Somehow poisoned by the product? No? Then leave this poor man alone and go on your way. You're ruining a perfectly amiable summer afternoon."

"How dare you," Cook sputtered. "Who do you think you are, woman? Trot on to bother someone else before—"

"I'd be careful on how you address Her Ladyship, the Countess of Trent." A strong arm circled Lily's waist as Owen gathered her safely behind him. She couldn't resist the smug thrill that ran through her at his protection and the priceless look of shock written on Sir Cook's face at learning her identity.

"My lord, my lady." He tapped his walking stick into the dirt a few times, bowing his head quickly in deference. "I apologize. Of course, I had no idea…"

"All women should be treated with respect… Sir Cook, is it? A gentleman should know this."

"Yes, yes. Quite right."

"I suggest you take your leave and think about your actions today, sir. As my wife said, you're ruining everyone's enjoyment."

Without another word, the man scampered away, leaving the parcel of contention behind on the vendor's counter, where the man promptly tossed it in a bin beside him. "Thank you, my lord, my lady. Please take whatever you'd like as a sign of my gratitude!"

"Oh, we couldn't. We only meted out justice. How dare he try to swindle you so blatantly!"

"It happens more often than you'd think, my lady."

"For that, I'm truly sorry." Lily tipped her head towards the assortment of candies. "Dear, why don't you purchase those collections of cinnamon sweets? I know they're your favorite."

Owen grinned as he laid out an extravagant amount of coins to the vendor's astonishment before snatching up the treats. An image of a toddler wearing a matching grin of mischief popped into her head, and she covered the slight bump of her belly.

Their child would have a sweet tooth like their father.

And the similarity brought a burst of joy to her heart.

"Shall we return to our original plan of ices or will candy suffice for now?" Owen asked, proffering one of the round delicacies.

Popping it into her mouth, Lily grinned. "The baby and I prefer both."

A bark of laughter drew the attention of those around them as they retreated to the back of the queue again. Lily loved his laugh, and she loved being the source of it even more.

Most of her acerbic comments or sassy remarks resulted in exasperated sighs from her family. It rapidly became too much for them. But never for Owen.

The Italian vendor manning the stall welcomed them forward and offered strawberry or marmalade ices. Lily noted a large container behind him where a woman and boy stirred and turned various metal cannisters, making enough of the flavors to keep up with demand.

"Two strawberries, please." Of course, Owen would remember her favorite fruit and guess her preference correctly. It concerned her how well he understood her, how attuned to her desires he was.

Not as if you can't do the same. Recall the cinnamon sweets of not ten minutes ago.

But for some reason, it didn't feel the same. Owen's knowledge attributed to his kindness. Hers... well, wasn't. Because she didn't think of herself as a particularly kind person—or at least one who possessed it as a defining quality.

"A penny for your thoughts." Owen bumped her elbow with his as they meandered through the crowd until they reached a grassy area where a group of children played. They seemed to be racing each other as two would line up before a third would drop a worn hanky to send them off to cross a makeshift finish line.

Searching for an appropriate replacement for her true thoughts, she asked, "Do you remember when we used to play tag as children?" She nodded towards the young group before them. A split had occurred, with boys on one side and girls on the other.

"Vividly. You and Hazel always won when we played as pairs."

"And I bet I could still beat you in a race." Though he certainly hadn't let himself go with age. Defined muscles flexed and trembled beneath his skin, and she knew most intimately the strength of his body. His arms bracing her against the wall. His chest bearing down on hers.

Goodness gracious!

Lily swallowed the last liquid sip of strawberry ice thankfully, her parched throat working double-time at the memory of exactly how *fit* her husband was.

"Care to a rematch?" He dared before glancing down at her belly. "If it's safe in your condition, that is."

"Surely, it's fine. My body's accustomed to a bit of exercise; it will be good for me."

"Excellent." They approached the crowd of children, and Owen interrupted whatever disagreement they were having with a jaunty smile. "Good day, children. May I trouble you for some help? My wife has challenged me to a footrace, and I can't deny the opportunity to claim a victory. Would you mind standing witness?"

Mouths agape, one boy moved forward. "Did you say you're going to race your wife? Aren't you the Earl of Trent?"

"Which makes my wife the Countess of Trent. Yes, you heard correctly." Owen winked at her, and she shook her head, bemused. "Are lords and ladies not allowed to participate in your fun?"

"Oh, no, sir! I didn't mean—"

"Ignore my husband's teasing, dear," Lily said, patting the flabbergasted boy on the shoulder. "He can't help himself. I'm

AN EARL LIKE ANY OTHER

only recently a countess, but before our marriage, I was just like you. A country lass who loved to scamper about outdoors."

Twin girls with red braids tittered behind their hands and scampered closer. "You're like Cinderella!"

Ah, miniature Hazels with their fanciful tales of romance. But she didn't find it as annoying as she may have in the past. In fact, it was sort of endearing.

"But I don't have an evil stepmother, thank heavens! Or terrible sisters, either!" Lily made a show of removing her boots, wiggling her toes within thin stockings—poor things sure to be torn from their upcoming trial—and beckoned for Owen to join her. "No excuses now, since I've chosen to give you an advantage by forgoing my sturdier boots. Are we ready to race or not, Mr. Prince Charming?"

"Boys, pay attention. A smart man would recognize that tone from his lady and gracefully bow out, ceding her superiority in every way. However, I've been accused of being slow in the past, so I fear I can't resist rising to this challenge." Owen grinned at her despite the conversation he referenced being hostile. That day at the gazebo seemed ages ago, certainly more than a mere matter of months.

And she supposed it hadn't been a completely terrible day; they'd shared their first kiss in years in that charged moment. The catalyst to their subsequent actions at his mother's ball.

Something I should regret, she reminded herself. *Stop ruminating on the past. You're having fun; don't ruin it!*

"Watch and learn girls," Lily countered, waving the little ones in fluttering pastel dresses to observe from the side. "Whenever a male supposes your inferiority based on your sex, be sure to show him the right of things with a prompt demonstration of your skills."

More giggles erupted from their young *students* as Lily and Owen took their places beside each other. Feeling the urge to laugh herself, she gave into the bit of joy and channeled it into an impulsive kiss on Owen's cheek. Immediately, he straightened from his hunched position, a flash of wonder causing her to flush from more than just excitement and the heat of the day.

It felt good to allow herself some freedom. To openly express herself without recriminations. Something about the euphoric atmosphere and their innocent onlookers must be catching, because the years of animosity melted away until it was just Lily and Owen—childhood friends and young lovers. Two individuals who fought and made up in equal measure. Two people who didn't bear the weight of costly mistakes.

"On your mark. Get set. Go!" The hanky dropped and Lily took off, leaving a dazed Owen behind before quickly recovering. Yielding grass cushioned every foot fall, and wind swept through her braided hair, teasing out reckless strands of abandon.

Heavy thumping stamped in the background as Owen gained speed, but she knew he wouldn't catch her. She'd never lost a race to him, and not for a lack on his part. Throwing her hands up in victory, Lily crossed the yellow ribbon laid out as the finish line while whooping hollers barreled down on her.

Congratulatory exclamations followed with each child beaming and sharing their enthusiasm at seeing a countess beat her earl. Their contagious energy drawing a laugh of pure joy from Lily.

"You were amazing, my lady!" A curly-haired tot exclaimed, her hand held securely in her older brother's. "How'd you learn to run that fast?"

Shifting into a comfortable position on the ground, Lily tucked her simple skirt under her knees while Owen sat beside her, lazily chewing on a blade of grass. Amusement gleamed from his grey eyes as he raised an eyebrow at her sudden popularity. Reveling in this unexpected sensation of happiness, she lowered a hand to his hidden in the grass and gently grazed her thumb back and forth before launching into tales of their adventures with her sisters.

Another vision bloomed in her mind. This time an idyllic scene of three. Her, Owen, and their child picnicking in the summer while they both told stories of their childhood.

And a peculiar thawing breached another one of her walls.

"I REMEMBER IT PERFECTLY because the sun bore down on my head like a blazing inferno, and later that evening my mother lamented the red crisp to my face." Owen crossed his arms in triumph, a victorious glow shining in his eyes, daring her to dispute the facts as he saw them.

After an afternoon spent entertaining the children and exploring the fair, they'd finished their tour on the outskirts of town, concealed in a forest of oaks. Cara and Iris had eaten lunch with them, while Owen's mother waved a greeting from her group of friends. All in all, it'd been one of the best days she'd had in a long time.

Invigorated, Lily gladly took up the gauntlet, determined to remind him exactly how wrong he was. *Must continue his losing streak after all*, she thought smugly. "Ah, yes, a blazing inferno of a day," she drawled. "Only the sky resembled a wooly gray blanket threatening to drench us in a deluge of rain at any second. But I understand how you could confuse the afternoon of our first kiss with another. As you liked to taunt, your true first kiss was with Sally Fielding, the butcher's daughter, under the oak tree behind her father's shop. On a perfectly sunny day."

A faint blush stained Owen's cheeks, and she relished the sight of his discomfiture until a sly grin transformed the look of chagrin into one of satisfaction. "And how is it, dear wife, that you recall such a memory? Jealous of Miss Fielding?"

"How is it, dear husband," she imitated. "That you've forgotten it? For weeks your crowing pestered those of us within earshot."

"I haven't forgotten it; the details were a bit off. Though to be fair, the day of our kiss, more enticing subjects interested me rather than the weather and location."

"Such as?"

Owen stalked forward, sudden heat darkening his irises, and it took all of Lily's strength to remain steadfast instead of retreating from his large form. "The way the bodice of your lavender gown molded to the high curve of your breasts. Wasn't the first time I'd noticed them, but it was the first time I saw a reciprocating appreciation in your eyes when I glanced upward. Tell me, what were you thinking?"

Lily weighed the consequences of speaking truthfully against lying, but what did it matter if he knew now?

"A wayward swath of hair kept falling into your eyes, it tempted me to brush it aside... which led to thoughts of what your cheek would feel like under my fingertips."

"Like the tender inside of a petal. That's what I imagined yours would be like, but I was wrong."

Her breath hitched in her lungs. Trying to make light of the dangerous direction their conversation headed, she asked, "I suppose it was more comparable to sandpaper or thistle?"

His quick laugh swept over her senses, rousing old memories of times they laughed after ridiculous spats. "Hardly. You're softer than any flower, Lily-pad."

A flutter beat against her belly, though whether from the babe or an unfortunate sprout of desire, she couldn't say.

"And the softest, sweetest part?" His voice dropped lower to form a cocoon of intimacy around them in the copse of trees. "The most tempting delicacies were these lips and the pretty pout, right here." His finger didn't touch, just hovered over her mouth. "But you were determined to remain ornery that day, weren't you? To make me chase?"

"Everything's come so easily for you, my lord," she taunted, knowing how he hated it when she became deferential. "A little effort didn't seem amiss at the time."

"I didn't say I didn't like it. Nothing worth having is easy to achieve."

"And you considered me worthy?"

"Correction: you're still worthy."

Oh, my.

Resting one hand above her head on the rough tree bark, he leaned forward, determination written on his handsome features. "Let's call a truce, shall we? We each made mistakes in the past, but we're adults now. It's not too late to build a future we both will be happy with, especially with a child on the way. I'm tired of the animosity between us, aren't you?"

Yes.

He mirrored her exact thoughts of the morning.

But could it really be that easy? Declaring a truce, moving on like none of it had happened?

"Think about it; I'll even help you." Owen rubbed his cheek against hers before blowing a stream of warm air across her neck underneath her ear, teasing the tendrils of hair that had escaped her braid. His tongue drew patterns on her skin before his lips sucked on the spot, surely leaving behind a trail of small bruises leading straight to her décolletage.

Breathless, Lily squirmed beneath him. "This is supposed to help me think? Funny, I don't recall this particular method for concentration."

"No?" He nipped at her bottom lip. "Must have picked it up on my travels, then."

They hadn't kissed since the short peck he'd given her at their wedding ceremony, which she hardly counted. The last true kiss between them had been on the fateful night of his mother's birthday ball—the night she got pregnant.

Suddenly, she wanted this more than anything. Wanted to wipe the slate clean. To erase that memory of frenzy and hurt and betrayal.

"Owen... Kiss me."

"Does this mean you agree?" He taunted, avoiding her searching mouth as she turned her head. "We agree to start anew and leave the past in the past."

"Yes, yes... Now, stop prolonging this torture and kiss me."

"As my lady wishes." A raffish grin blinked into view before her eyes closed to the brightness of the moment, and they sealed their deal with a kiss. Skimming eager hands up his body, she relished the feel of shifting muscles beneath his clothing. Relished the fact that she could stop pretending not to want him as desperately as she did.

A low groan rumbled between them as Owen laid his weight more heavily into hers, pressing her harder against the massive tree trunk. Scrapes of bark dug into her skin. Then a waft of heat tore her focus from discomfort to shock.

"I've wanted to do this for months." The neckline of her dress flapped in the wind after Owen unlaced the ties holding it together. She'd worn a simple peasant top for the fair, nothing ornate to befit her recent title, and it provided easy access for her husband's roving hands as he slid the last barrier between them—her flimsy chemise—aside, tugging it to rest below her breasts. Hefting the globes in his rough palms, Owen tested their weight with a squeeze, but her abrupt inhale stopped him cold.

"What's the matter? Did I hurt you?"

"Hurt's a bit strong." She nibbled her lip, embarrassed by this new discovery of her ever-changing body. "But they are sore, sensitive. It's the baby's fault." And she had not an ounce of guilt for blaming the little one either.

"Ah... I'll be gentler, then."

Delicate kisses peppered her breasts, following freckles and veins haphazardly, until Owen took a swollen nipple between his lips and suckled—tenderly, rhythmically—the sensual pull creating a direct pulsing below.

"Owen..." His name hung in the air as he switched sides. The indecent sound of wet flesh meeting in an erotic symphony shivered through her senses.

"Is this alright, sweetheart?" Hazel gold clashed with flashing silver as their gazes met over her breast, the nipple remaining indecently inside Owen's mouth, cheeks hollowing at each light suck.

A trembling nod answered him, and a warm hand ventured under her skirt. Another clothing item meant for comfort on a hot summer day, it allowed him easy access to the treasure he searched for.

"Owen, we shouldn't..." His palm cupped her quim. Bracing her heels in the ground, Lily canted forward, yearning for a firmer touch. "We could get caught."

"Excellent point, darling." He traced her outer lips, combing through wet curls, before sliding through her slick heat. "It's about damn time we gave everyone a different scandal to remember. Whenever your name enters a conversation, I want mine attached to it, not that fucking Asa Lynch." A sharp thrust of fingers punctuated his point, and Lily squeaked at the swift entry.

Withdrawing with a wicked suctioning, Owen repeated the harsh plunge again, the heel of his palm smacking her clitoris, and making her buck in response.

"Oh, god..."

"Can you imagine the gossip, especially from that nosy body, Mrs. Holly?" He nipped her ear, lost in passion. "The Earl of Trent caught fucking his countess against a tree. Her wet pussy squeezing his fingers with each rough thrust. Her cries of need only assuaged when he sank his cock into her waiting heat."

"Mrs. Holly learned some filthy words since I last saw her," Lily muttered, clamping intimate muscles on Owen's fingers to entice him to follow through with his story.

"You have no idea..." His pace quickened, each upward stroke grinding into the tingling bud of her sex. "Damn, you could kill a man with this cunt. You're doing so well, Lily-pad. Are you going to take my cock so easily? I warn you, it's thick. I'm going to stretch you, darling. Won't you like that?"

"Yes..." She moaned as her orgasm rose like a tidal wave, crashing through her senses and carrying her away from everything but Owen. It had been ages since she'd felt such a release. Since Owen and their trysts.

His touch gentled, drawing out the sensations until the little spasms in her muscles subsided. "I remember how large you are, Owen. I've dreamt about that day we swam in the lake numerous times." Too many times, if she were honest. But she always woke before the culmination of their kisses and touches.

Now, it was his turn to pant with pleasure. Light eyes bore into hers. "Have you? When was the last time?"

"Three days ago. After I caught you returning from another swim. Your shirt hung over your shoulders. Bold of you to let the maids see you so undone." Like a dog with its tongue hanging out, she'd watched from the parlor window as he traipsed up the drive, desperate to lick the droplets of water shining under the sun, gilding his skin in diamonds.

"Jealous?"

Lily kissed a path up his neck, reveling in the salty sweat, before admitting, "Quite."

"Next time, you'll have to join me."

Licking her lips, she retied the laces on her shirt and shimmied out from under Owen before replying with a wink. "Maybe I will." She exaggerated the swing of her hips, knowing he tracked her every move like a hungry predator.

"And you'll be naked this time, won't you?" Their previous swimming interlude she'd held onto her propriety by the scrap of her chemise.

"I can hardly swim with layers weighing me down, can I?" Lily teased, arching a brow as her head tilted to catch his pained expression as he caught up to her. He must be imagining it. Gaze dropping to his groin, she already knew he was worked up from fingering her, but it appeared he'd swelled more with her taunts.

She should take pity on him.

Should relieve him.

It wouldn't be a hardship. Her hand itched to remember the velvety skin of his shaft, the heavy stones beneath. It had been ages since she'd felt those as well.

"Then you're definitely joining me, minx." Suddenly, Owen's hands attacked her sides, determined to tickle and grab, a playful growl emanating from his chest. Yelping at the abrupt attack, Lily skipped away with a laugh.

"What do you think you're doing?"

"Capturing my wife, so she can stop tormenting me with fantasies." He lunged for her again, but Lily was too quick, jogging just out of his reach.

"We're too old to play this game, Owen." But that didn't stop her from provoking him, edging closer before bounding away with a giggle. As if time had reversed, they acted like teenagers again, running and hollering, teasing the other, and if someone happened to witness the antics of the local earl and his wife, they would've smiled, remarking upon what a lovely pair the two lovebirds made.

CHAPTER THIRTEEN

We've started anew, and I'm finally brave enough (on paper) to admit how much I adore you. Why is it easier to express myself through ink than my voice? You know well enough how direct I am in all other matters.

NIGHTS WERE LONG AND days short as weeks passed in relative peace. With a truce declared and the intimacy at the fair lingering in their minds, Owen and Lily spent the evenings relearning each other. Slow and sensual. With the other's care uppermost in their mind.

A vast difference from their original coupling at his mother's ball, and a hindrance to their current situation of not having reached a complete consummation of their marriage yet. Thus, he enjoyed morning breakfasts with his wife where she regaled him with her latest dreams—vivid and outlandish, courtesy of the baby, she insisted—and evening suppers filled with his explanation of the latest work being done on the estate.

However, the snail-like pace began to wear on him.

Owen had no idea how to approach his wife about his need. After all, if the situation didn't bother her, it shouldn't bother him. Like a good husband, he should keep letting her lead in the bedroom. They could continue in the current vein, content and amiable—if not fully sated.

Rubbing tired eyes, Owen cursed the ledger in front of him for the fifth time as he reread the numbers. Focusing was becoming more difficult by the day, it seemed, because distractions abounded around every corner.

Lily's favorite scent lingering in the hall.

A pair of languorous silk gloves forgotten on a table.

Or the yellow piece of ribbon he kept hidden in his desk, stolen from his wife's vanity after their day at the fair.

She surrounded him without any effort at all, yet a distance remained.

"Excuse me, sir. Mr. Michael Stilt, the land agent, is here to see you."

"Of course. Let him in." Owen stood to wave a stout man inside the study, directing him to the leather chair across from him. "How may I help you, Mr. Stilt?"

Removing his cap and nodding his head in respect, the man took a seat and began, "My lord, I'm afraid we have trouble on the southern parcel, near the Filcher's farm. A retaining wall has crumbled, allowing the river to flood the fields. Proper drainage is paramount, though their harvest in the fall will most likely suffer."

"I see." A nerve pinched in his jaw as his teeth ground together. Accidents like this happened all the time through no fault of anyone, but Owen felt like he was somehow responsible for the failing. Especially with all the incidents lately. First, the Henley beam falling on Garrett, which, thankfully, he survived. Now, a flood at the Filcher's.

AN EARL LIKE ANY OTHER

Perhaps he should've checked the strength of the wall at regular intervals instead of trusting its steadfastness. Perhaps he should've foreseen a flood and invested in whatever equipment would be necessary now to fix the problem.

Perhaps.
Maybe.
Should have.

Stilt continued speaking, explaining next steps, requesting permission for certain purchases while Owen's mind retreated behind a gauze of self-recrimination. His father's warning leaping to the forefront.

Do better for the family. Improve the family legacy.

Which means not allowing distractions of your wife to interfere with estate work.

Surreptitiously, he opened the drawer to his right and drew the yellow ribbon into his lap, winding the silky fabric between his fingers. The repetitive act calmed him, grounded him in a way nothing else could have at that moment.

When Stilt stared as if waiting for a response, Owen briskly nodded and stood to shake the man's hand. "Yes, I agree. Please see that everything is done as hastily as possible. Good day."

After the man's departure, Owen followed at a sedate pace, needing fresh air to blow away the cobwebs in his brain, but a familiar tied scroll caught his attention in the entryway. Why hadn't Marvin notified him of a second message?

He'd almost forgotten the first one in the intervening weeks. Stuffing Lily's ribbon in his coat pocket, he ripped the missive open and scanned the scribbled writing.

Your tainted marriage brings your father shame.

Who the bloody hell had the gall to send him such tripe? When he discovered the author, he promised they'd rue the day they decided to play this game. Though what its end could be, he had no clue.

Clearly, they had some relationship with his father. Or at least knew their family history well enough to guess a joining of the former earl's son and their neighboring daughter wouldn't have been ideal.

This is exactly what I needed to top off the afternoon.

More ammunition added to his fear of never living up to his father's standards. Of letting him down with his poor decision-making.

"My lord, do you need something?" A passing maid paused in her chore to question him, curiosity coloring her cheeks. He must look like a right dolt standing in the hallway, still as a statue, fist clenched around the ugly parchment.

"Do you know where the countess is?"

After learning of his wife's whereabouts, his booted feet unerringly headed upstairs—a craving for the comfort of her presence spurring him forward.

THE QUIET CLICK OF the door signaled someone's arrival, and Lily prayed the intruder wouldn't disturb Zinnia, who lay curled up by her side on the bed. She kept butting her head against Lily's arm, eyes closed, still napping, yet searching to be closer.

"I don't think she can get any nearer." Owen whispered, coming into view. Sunlight gilded his auburn hair with a golden halo as he shrugged out of his jacket, ruffling the velvety layers.

"It's adorable and sweet how close she wants to get."

"When you love someone, you can never get close enough." Lily and Owen's eyes met over the napping feline—a wordless understanding passing between them—and a pleasant heat seeped into her bones, like the last rays of summer soaking the earth, rooting deep underground.

"Shouldn't you be resting, too?" Boots removed and shirt loosened from its mooring at his waist, he looked tousled and oh-so-touchable—to the point where Lily's fingers twitched in their previously languid position.

"I've tried, but I can't resist watching her. Whiskers twitching and nose burrowing into me."

Owen rounded the end of the bed before the mattress dipped, and his body mirrored hers across from Zinnia, chest to chest, with a ball of fur in between.

Breathless at his unexpected nearness, she asked, "What are you doing?"

"Helping you rest, too. Maybe it'll be easier to sleep if someone's cuddling and petting you, as well." His arm covered hers, fingers tracing over the bare skin, gently scratching Zinnia's ear, before returning to mark a soothing path from Lily's neck to shoulder, all the way down to her fingertips.

"You're going to disturb her with all this movement," she warned, despite yearning for more of his touch.

"She doesn't look perturbed in the least. You, on the other hand..." A sensual twinkle entered Owen's gaze as he continued to caress her. Massaging the juncture of her neck and shoulder. Circling her temple with his thumb. Like the sleeping feline,

Lily felt like purring under his undivided attention. "Look positively disheveled," he finished with a groan.

His hand tangled with her loose braid before closing the gap between them. Questing lips glided over hers—once, twice—molding perfectly to the lush curves. Their breaths mingled in the quiet, humid and heavy with each drawn-out kiss, an intimate convergence that slowed the blood in Lily's veins to the viscosity of molasses. Cinnamon melted on her tongue, and she moaned at the familiar spice.

Owen and his sweets, she thought fondly.

"I missed your kisses while I was gone." The confession sent her heart skittering into an awkward gallop of skipped beats as she secretly admitted the same. "Thankfully, we created a stockpile of them to remember all those times at the gazebo. You've no idea how often I carried those with me, warming myself with their heat, even during the dead of winter in the Swiss Alps."

Tracing the bold line of his nose before tapping his mouth with a fingertip, Lily said, "I'm surprised I featured in your mind at all. Weren't you trying to escape everything from Shoreham? Your father's death and my betrayal?"

"You underestimate how much I loved you."

An arrow buried itself deep in her chest at his use of the past tense. *Loved*. Not love.

Of course, he doesn't harbor love for you. It's been years, and the two of you are only just coming to terms with friendship again.

"Despite what you thought of me? It couldn't have been a favorable opinion," she pressed.

"No, it wasn't." He said it without rancor, but that didn't lessen the shame she felt. "But I also couldn't shut my heart off so easily. One indiscretion apparently fails to eclipse eighteen years of familiarity and affection."

"I'll remember that in another eighteen years when you try reminding me of something from this year."

Sighing, his hand traveled down to her belly, more pronounced these days. "Eighteen years. Can you imagine? We'll have an adult on our hands."

"Barely." She winced, recalling the terrible mistakes she made at that age.

"Have you thought of a name yet?" As if hearing its future being decided, the baby kicked at Owen's palm, causing them both to jolt. Zinnia didn't like the sudden movement and stretched her four legs before sauntering down to the end of the bed, away from the disturbing humans.

"How long has that been happening?" Awe colored Owen's tone as he shifted forward, placing his hand here and there, trying to feel the kick again.

"Not too long. Every time it happens, I'm about to call for you when it stops. But she must want a say in her name."

"Ivy. Petunia. Maple." Owen spit out the litany of names. No kicks. "Rose. Tulip. Chrysanthemum."

"Chrysanthemum?" Lily giggled at the outrageous suggestion.

"In keeping with the Garden Girl tradition, of course."

Impulsively, she pressed a light kiss to his mouth in gratitude. It was sweet how he wanted to honor her family's naming conventions. "What if it's a boy? Perhaps, that's why you're not getting a positive response."

"Hmm, you may be onto something... William, Henry, Christopher."

"All's quiet on the baby front." She patted his hand in consolation. "But don't worry, four months lie between us and parenthood, so there's plenty of time to figure it out."

"I suppose you're right." He tightened an arm around her, shortening the empty space between them. "How are you feeling about that?"

Lily considered his question. Should she tell him the truth? Would he be as ashamed of her as she was of herself?

Afraid to learn the truth, she lied. "I feel as every expectant mother does." Vague but good enough for Owen, it seemed, as he pressed another kiss to her lips. This time she grabbed the back of his neck and held him there, worried he'd try to continue the line of conversation.

And because you can't get enough of his touch.

Yes, because she craved her husband's kisses for as long as he'd give them to her.

CHAPTER FOURTEEN

Azalea. Calla. Dahlia.
Lucas. Matthew. George.
I thought I felt a flutter around Lucas, but we shall see...

AS LUNCHEONS WENT, Lily didn't think it could be worse.

Iris and Cara flanked her, the three sisters watching in horror as Asa Lynch strode through the party looking for all the world like he belonged there and hadn't ruined Lily's reputation seven years prior.

Please be a hallucination.

Though she knew it unlikely based on the matching looks of shock painted on her sisters' faces, the tiniest possibility remained, considering Lily could've sworn she'd seen Mr. Laramie skittering through the party earlier. Which made about as much sense as her past liaison's current presence.

"What on earth is he doing here? Doesn't he work for a family in Derbyshire now?" Nothing like the ghosts of mistakes past to rise again and wreak havoc on her life. Everything had been going too well since her and Owen's truce. It was only right for fate to throw Asa back in her face.

And for him to appear at the last public event I'm attending before going into confinement.

"His mother must have invited him for a visit, and he decided to join her today. It's the only explanation, because I doubt he cares about the parsonage's new roof." The purpose of the day's function was to celebrate the generous benefactors who'd provided the funds for said roofing, particularly the Earl and Countess of Trent, thus her and Owen's presence.

"Is he daft? What possible good does he think could come from flaunting around these parts while Lily's a countess now. She has Owen's protection and reviving the scandal could only bring negative light to himself." Iris rightly pointed out, sipping the tepid tea in her cup.

"Well, he lied about what happened in the first place, so I wouldn't bank on his stock of common sense." Honestly, what had she been thinking of choosing him as the man to use for breaking things off with Owen? "Perhaps he likes the spotlight, however fractured and tainted it may be."

"Oh, dear!" Cara waved her fan vigorously, shooting her wayward curls askew. "He's coming this way. The absolute nerve!"

Girding herself for the forthcoming conversation, Lily straightened her shoulders and searched for her husband in the crowd. She didn't want him to catch them together, no matter how innocent the exchange.

"Ah, the infamous Garden Girls! How lovely to see you all." Usually not one for fanfare, Lily resisted correcting his improper address as he didn't even mention her improved status in society.

"Mr. Lynch."

"Pardon my interruption, but there's a matter of importance I must discuss with her ladyship." He had the audacity to wink at her. *The impertinent, uncouth...*

"I'm not certain that is wise, sir. Given the circumstances."

An agreement stuttered to a halt on Lily's lips. It occurred to her that this might be her only opportunity to learn why Lynch had lied about their liaison. To finally know the whole sordid story that had spun out of her control.

"Don't worry, dear. Five minutes won't blacken my name anymore that it has been. Shall we take a turn about the garden?" Without waiting for a response, she turned in her slippers and left her sisters gaping after them while the hurried footsteps of Lynch followed closely behind.

Waist length hedges sat in orderly rows of flourishing green, white, and red, providing a suitable amount of privacy while keeping them in full view of guests. She would not be caught alone with the bounder.

"Say what you have to say, for I have questions of my own for you to answer," she snipped, infusing her voice with all the frostiness of a bored monarch.

"Is that anyway to treat an old friend, Lil?"

She abhorred that nickname. "You will address me in a way befitting the Countess of Trent. *My lady* will do just fine."

"Come on, Lil." She wondered how much pressure it took to break a tooth as her molars ground together. *Insufferable man.* "It's me. Surely, I deserve better than cold disregard."

He truly was mad.

"*Surely*, you say." Her fingers wound around her folded fan and a temptation to whack him over the head with it bolted down her arm. Oh, how she'd love to witness his reaction to being so thoroughly walloped. "As I recall, we shared a peck on the lips—I'd hardly qualify it as a legitimate embrace—when you decided to embellish to the point of blatant falsehoods. Implying I'd given you my virtue. Ruining my reputation. Making me a pariah for years to come. What part of being a lying, scheming bastard deserves anything more than a swift kick to your groin?"

Massive amounts of oxygen filled her lungs as she huffed in righteous anger. The nerve of this man!

"Still a little spitfire, I see." Lynch chuckled—ignoring her insults, her threats—instead daring to grab her arm and trap her between two arches at the end of the row, shielding them from view.

"Unhand me, you mongrel." She ripped her arm out of his grip. The joy of finally letting loose the store of names she'd imagined calling him if they ever met again sent a rush of satisfaction straight to her head. Ladies, especially countesses, didn't speak so plainly, but she wasn't in polite company at the moment.

No, an unrepentant leech stood before her instead.

Her hatred seemed to penetrate Lynch's congenial facade at long last as his eyes narrowed. "Don't pretend you didn't enjoy our kiss. And don't act as if you didn't want more. No self-respecting woman throws herself at a man without wanting a bit of a slap and tickle. I'm just here to make good on all those implications."

"You must be truly delusional if you think for one moment I would ever allow you to touch me again. The fact that I let your despicable mouth near mine is a regret I'll have for the rest of my life, if only I could scrub the memory away."

AN EARL LIKE ANY OTHER

Brows furrowing in anger, his hands snatched her by the shoulders and shoved her against the stone arch at her back. Fear should've entered at this point, but Lily's fury was too ferocious. Smacking her fan against his face, she tried to fight him off. "Release me at once! When Owen discovers what you've done, he'll—"

Lynch laughed in her face, an ugly sound that grated on her ears. "Ha! Your precious earl? What will he do? Escape to France again? Spain? He won't do anything because he doesn't care about you. He didn't then either, or else he wouldn't have run like a bloody jackrabbit."

"Don't you dare insult him, you—"

"Darling, I can fight my own battles, but I do appreciate the effort." A deceivingly calm drawl came from behind Lynch, and Lily sagged in relief at Owen's arrival, then tensed as she imagined how this scene must look to him. Her, alone again with Lynch. Just like before.

Except this time your lips aren't pressed together in a paltry facsimile of betrayal.

"As for you." He ripped Lynch backwards, tossing the man to the grass. "If you ever come near my wife again, I will use all the power infused in me by the Queen of England to ensure you never step foot on English soil again. Do I make myself clear?"

Lynch scoffed. The man really was an imbecile. "You may be a lord, but I don't kowtow to no one. Least of all a man satisfied with taking my sloppy seconds."

She gasped at the insinuation, blanching at the damning words.

Owen dragged Lynch up by the collar before slamming him into the arch she'd previously been trapped against. "Fucking bastard!" A swift fist to Lynch's gut bent the man over double. "You dare to dishonor my wife, the bloody Countess of Trent, the woman carrying my child to my face?" His knee drove upward, straight into Lynch's nose, and she winced at the resounding crunch of bone.

Agony written on his crumpled features, Asa fell to the ground, clutching a bloody nose. "You broke it!" He howled in pain, and a crowd began to circle them.

"That won't be the last thing I break if I see you again. Heed my warning this time. Get the fuck out of Hampshire before I have you shipped to the colonies in Australia." Threat delivered, Owen whipped around to brace an arm around Lily's back and usher her to privacy, allowing gossip to circulate unhindered behind them.

"Owen..."

"Don't. Say. A. Fucking. Word." A shuddering breath ran through him. "I... I'm trying to control myself after seeing Lynch again."

Tears rose unbidden as her mouth trembled in silence.

This was the man from before.

The man who loathed her.

The man she'd betrayed.

"Why did you let me believe you slept with Lynch?" Owen asked, dropping his hold on her like it was a hot coal burning his hand. He'd led her to their carriage where he'd promptly instructed their driver to take them home.

On opposite sides of the closed conveyance, a sense of relief seemed contrary to the situation, but to finally have this

AN EARL LIKE ANY OTHER

conversation once and for all comforted her. They'd broached it a couple of times, usually in anger, neither of them ever able to stay calm enough to have it out.

The few times they had managed to control themselves, they'd been interrupted.

Now it appeared—calm or not—they would finish this.

"It was for the best."

"How do you figure? Was it for the best when I couldn't stomach staying in Shoreham to comfort my mother after my father's death? Was it for the best that I'd lost my best friend and lover in one fell swoop? Or perhaps you're referring to the night I took your maidenhead against a damn wall?" The lethality of his words escalated until he pinned Lily with a harsh stare, daring her to refute him.

Swallowing the lump in her throat, Lily repeated her reasoning. "It needed to be done." Remembered frustration welled inside her gut, heightening her own ire at his naivete. "It was naïve of us to believe an earl's son could marry a professor's daughter, a nobody. We were too young and idealistic." Her disgusted snipe clearly chafed his already raw nerves as his nostrils flared like a bull seeing red. "I did what had to be done; what you couldn't do."

"What you did was decide that it wouldn't work between us and took it upon yourself to ruin your reputation. Don't think I haven't heard the stories coming out of the village. Servants talk. You decided that this was all for me? Horse shite! You did it for yourself because you were scared."

"I'm not afraid of anything, least of all what gossip mongers in the village say. I was the stronger of the two of us then."

"You truly believe that, don't you?" Amazement painted his features. "Orchestrating a childish scheme to break things off while casting yourself in the muck. A strong person would've told me outright that you wanted out."

"And you would have accepted such a declaration? You're as delusional as Lynch if that's what you believe." Why couldn't he see? She'd done what needed to be done for them to go on with their lives without prolonging the inevitable heartbreak. *Except you did the exact opposite. You extended everything out another seven bloody years.*

"Don't compare me to him. I'm a gentleman, a damned lord of the realm! I've never forced a woman in my life. If you cared nothing for me, you could've said so instead of stomping my heart into the dust like a bug under your boot."

"Can't you see? I did care for you. I loved you, for goodness's sake! If I tried to lie to your face, you would have seen right through me, and we would have remained together no matter the consequences. No matter how the relationship between you and your parents would've been affected."

"My parents never expected me to..." A beseeching look overcame his features as he bent forward, elbows propped on his knees.

"Don't patronize me, Owen. Of course, they did. You forget I know your family's history. They liked me, yes, but would they truly have wanted me as a daughter-in-law? Your father, who was already trying to overcome his father's tainted past? No, and that's the truth. What then?"

"We would have married, like we are now, with my mother adoring you. We ended up in the same position, only with years of pain and distrust between us instead of love and affection.

Thanks to you," he bit out, a red hue of anger highlighting his cheeks.

A jolt shook the carriage as a sharp retort froze on her tongue.

They were home.

Lily didn't wait for Owen to exit before ambling down herself to the surprise of the footman holding the door aloft. Avoiding the house, she headed towards the stables, needing the innocent kittens to soothe her frayed nerves. Zinnia had given birth to a litter of three over a week ago, and she needed their sweet temperament to settle her raging emotions.

"Where are you going? We're not done yet."

"I'd prefer to not announce our issues to the entire staff. Is that too much to ask, your lordship?"

"Christ, you infuriating woman!" His heavy marching pounded the path behind her, and she expelled a breath of relief at seeing the empty stables. The stable-hands, nowhere to be found.

"Do you think if I'd known we'd end up in this farce of a marriage after all this time that I would've continued with my plan? Do you think I have a sadistic need to inflict as much pain as possible on myself and others? What a terrible wife you've tied yourself to." Swiping at her watery eyes, Lily hurried to a stall at the end and swung open the gate to approach Zinnia and her babies, safe in a fresh bed of hay.

"Hello, darlings. I'm afraid I'm in need of your comfort," she murmured. Unfortunately, they were napping instead of awake and ready to jump into her needy arms. Reluctant to disturb their sleeping forms, Lily knelt in the hay to run gentle fingertips over their silky coats, the contact giving her a semblance of peace.

It's just another argument with Owen. You'll get through this.

But her emotions boiled too close to the surface, threatening to spill over to splash and burn everything in its wake. Her skin itched. Her heart thumped like the battle drums at Waterloo.

A helpless growl stuck in Owen's chest, and he slammed a fist against a wooden plank in the wall, spooking one of the mares. Apologizing to the poor animal, Owen watched Lily from outside the gate.

"Of course not. But I have noticed your penchant to view life through something akin to black-tinted glasses." The fury deflated in him as she watched the transformation from tense and hunched to looser but confused, his expressive features arranging themselves in a gentler emotion.

"Is it any wonder why? My life's a shambles."

"Hardly. You have loving sisters. You're a countess. You can have anything you want if you only ask."

Lily carefully stood to her feet and left the cats to their nap. She'd interrupted their sleep enough. Pacing from stall to stall, her long braid swung down her back—wayward strands sticking out all over her head after falling loose from its earlier coronet—fists opening and closing as she tried to quell the raging storm inside.

"You don't understand. At any moment, everything can change, disappear. Seven years ago, I made a decision and fate decided to punish me for it in a never-ending cycle of negative karma. Lynch serves as a perfect example! Why else would he randomly appear in our lives again?"

Shaking her head in frustration, Lily tried to cuddle the curious head of a mare who peeked over the door caging her in, but the horse immediately shifted away, escaping her needy clutch.

Even this gentle beast can't stand to be near me.

"Everything's been wrong since Lynch and my parents' deaths, then losing you and almost the house. I can't get past it." A sob broke through the anger masking the deep well of sadness inside her. "Something's wrong with me, something unfixable."

"Nonsense. What can I do?" Owen asked, hesitantly moving closer, the fiery battle earlier forgotten in the wake of her brokenness. "I hate seeing you cry."

"Probably not as much as I hate crying." A trembling hand smoothed over her cheeks. "I'm just so sad. And so angry I could scream."

"Then scream, but not in here or you'll scare the horses." Catching one of her hands, she found herself being led by Owen for the second time that day. "But we can go to the lake."

"Changing scenery won't fix me. I'm not good, Owen. I don't deserve you or any of this." A sweep of her arm encompassed the surrounding estate: grand mansion, rolling hills, and the lake beyond the tree line.

"What are you talking about?"

"There's a reason these bad things keep happening to me."

"Your sisters lost their parents, too, sweetheart."

"Yes, but I'm the one who brought shame and scandal. I'm the one who tore me and you apart. Even Mr. Laramie chose me to marry! Something inside me drew him in—the wicked part." Lost in her tirade, a familiar refrain that played in her mind on the darkest of nights, she continued, "I'm not sweet or kind like Iris or as self-sacrificing as Cara. I'm selfish. I'm mean. Aren't you tired of me yet? Rude, rash—I'm nothing like that girl you used to know."

Owen tilted his head to the side as they traipsed over rocks and old, brittle leaves along the forest floor. "Really..." A challenging twinkle entered his eyes. "Because the girl I remember had that same attitude of defiance, even if she wasn't quite so melancholic or self-pitying."

"It's not self-pity if it's the truth."

"It's opinion. A very wrong opinion." They broke through the brush to a serene view of the lake, dark blue and glinting in the sunlight. "Now, strip to your chemise because we're going swimming."

"Now?" They were in the middle of an argument turned, well, essentially, it turned into her spilling her soul to him in a bid to show him every shadowy part of her. To make him see her as she was. As she knew herself to be.

"Yes. I think we can both use a cool down." Tan fingers flitted over Owen's clothing, unbuttoning and untying, while she stood dumbfounded, baffled by the swatches of skin being revealed. "Any day now, Lily-pad."

Sweat gathered on her brow, and a longing glance shot over the water, sure to be cool and refreshing. *You've already bared your soul. What's a little flesh?*

Besides, she wasn't one to shirk from an obvious dare.

Making quick work of her clothing, Lily kept her underthings on as a shield—a flimsy one, but a barrier nonetheless—and waited for her husband's next directive.

CHAPTER FIFTEEN

I must confess: I adore your protective nature. Is it barbaric of me to delight in your reactions when someone threatens me in the slightest?

OWEN TORE HIS HUNGRY eyes from Lily's exposed form, the cotton of her undergarments transparent in direct light. The bump of her belly drew forth a feeling of possessiveness so strong that a vision of hefting her into his arms and carrying her off to a darkened part of the forest materialized. They'd be alone, and he'd press her deep into the ground with his cock driving into her ripe body.

Clearing his throat, he shook the image away, forcing a facade of civility over his features. A fantasy for another day. With their outer layers shed, Owen guided them to the water's edge before they tiptoed forward, shivering at the sudden chill.

"Lay on your back and float. Let your mind release these dark thoughts you've been having and trust me to care for you whatever happens in the future. A future that you have no control over." He began, unsure of how exactly to help Lily overcome such strong emotions, but willing to try. Her need eclipsed the fury he'd felt seeing Lynch touching her at the luncheon. Hearing his insults. "Instead of letting the lack of control cause fear or anger, let it comfort you because it means at any moment there's an equal chance of things shifting for better as much as worse."

"I'm not sure it'll be that easy," she said, though her body obeyed the request as she leaned back. Wet cotton clung to her, outlining every curve and emphasizing the shadow of her nipples and the thatch of curls between her thighs. Desire warred with the platonic aid he was trying to deliver.

Unaware of his struggle, Lily continued, "The truth is, I've been acting out this way for a few years, and I don't know why. I hear myself being a harpy. I tell myself to stop, but it's like someone else is controlling my actions. I know I must release this anger somehow... It comes out in the harshest way possible, usually directed at my sisters or you."

She sighed. "But floating in a lake doesn't seem like it will fix the problem."

"Have you tried it yet, Lily-pad?"

"You and your ridiculous pet names," she muttered before saying, "No."

"The Garden Girls is catchy and undeniably fits. As does Lily-pad. When you're clever enough to come up with a suitable nickname for me, you won't hear a complaint."

"Oh, I have a couple of nicknames, alright."

"Appropriate names," he teased. "But back to possible solutions. If you've never tried this before, then you can't possibly know if it'll work or not. Just give it... give me a chance."

Speaking softly, Owen listed the things he admired most about her while she bobbed in the water before him.

"You challenge me more than anyone of my acquaintance. You see me as more than my title—see the true man beneath it all."

"You fight for justice. Always stepping in to defend those who can't defend themselves."

The gentle words continued, and soon tears slid from beneath her lashes to drip into the lake. "Damn whatever this baby has coursing through my blood. They make me a watering pot."

"This is good for you, even your walls can't combat physiology. It's forcing you to deal with your emotions, so they're no longer bottled."

"Well, you try crying at the drop of a hat and tell me how you like it. Salt stings, you know." He kept a steadying hand beneath her as she wiped at her eyes.

"Stop reducing yourself to some silly woman. You're more than that. You've endured real tragedies; these aren't *drop of a hat* tears."

"No, but this morning when I cried because my favorite dress wouldn't lace up anymore? Those were silly tears." He allowed her the victory, continuing to keep a bracing hand at her back for support.

They stayed in their positions for long minutes, until both of their breathing synced together, slowing and relaxing with each deep breath.

"Contrary to my previous opinion, I do feel better," Lily finally said. "Can we get out of the water now before we turn into raisins?"

"If you're ready, then yes." Helping her find her footing in the sinking mud underneath them, they waded to shore.

"Hopefully, no one's walking the forest or else they'll get an eyeful of my transparent chemise. Indecent, indeed."

"But very alluring. Like my own little water nymph." He brushed a knuckle over her raised nipples. "This may be one of my favorite looks of yours."

"IT WOULD BE," SHE SCOLDED playfully, pleasure seeping into her bones. Hoisting tired limbs to the verdant grass lining the lake edge, Lily collapsed to her back, throwing an arm over her eyes to shield herself from the blinding sun.

Somehow, Owen's wild notion of floating in the lake to release part of her pain seemed to have helped. Her mind and soul felt lighter—perhaps gray instead of black, she thought amusedly—which was more than she'd expected from the strange but tranquil interlude.

A yawn bubbled up—another effect of her pregnancy.

"Tired, sweetheart?"

Mumbled agreement slipped past her lips when a large hand wrapped around her ankle. Quaking in surprise, Lily propped herself up on her elbows to find Owen observing her with the strangest look on his face, his eyes fixated on her body.

"Lie back down." The husky command feathered lazily through the air before she cautiously obeyed.

Rough palms slid along her calves, smoothing up and down her legs, each time reaching higher until they pried the clinging hem of her chemise upward to rest at her waist.

Exposed. Vulnerable. *His.*

AN EARL LIKE ANY OTHER

"I'm going to share a secret with you, my dear. I'd never been with a woman before you. We were both virgins that night."

Shock—swift and powerful fired through her brain. Owen had been a virgin? Cold shame filtered through the shock as she remembered how she'd treated him. How callous she'd been. In so much pain that she'd inflicted it on Owen in retribution.

"I'm sorry."

"As am I... Except it's difficult to work up too much guilt when it gave me you as my wife. And our child, of course. But I do wish our first time had been less anger-fueled. Gentler. Loving." She felt his hands tighten around her hips. "Will you let me love you the way I've dreamed of?"

How could she refuse such an endearing request?

The answer? She couldn't.

"Yes..." One breathy word of acquiescence, but it was all he needed. Lowering his head, cool droplets of water fell to her skin as he peeled the cotton from her chest, revealing a berry nipple to the sun.

"Would it be too crass to admit how much I yearn to taste your milk after the baby's born?"

He... what? The idea never occurred to her that he—or anyone would want to do such a thing—but as his lips wrapped around a taut bud and suckled, she found herself longing to satisfy his curiosity.

"You can do whatever you want with me. Nothing is too much." Owen would never harm her, which meant he could only ever please her with his sexual fantasies. They could explore the possibilities together like they truly were those teenagers in love.

Groaning at her admission, Owen worked his way south, biting her through the chemise at her hip, circling her pushed out belly button. "You shouldn't give me carte blanche, love. I might take advantage."

"A nobleman? An earl like you? Never."

He paused in his ministrations to meet her lust-filled gaze. "I'm an earl like any other, Lily. A man like any other."

"Except you're not," she refuted. "You married me: a simple country girl. Half of your blood is Irish. You aren't like any other earl in all of England."

His head dropped. A deep rumble vibrated in his chest. "When you say things like that... Fuck..."

Spreading her fingers through his damp hair, Lily coaxed him to look at her again as she teased. "Mrs. Holly wasn't the only one whose language has gotten filthier, it seems. I don't remember quite as many curses leaving your mouth in our youth."

"I didn't know as many, then. The Continent was rather enlightening. And all of my filters disappear around you. So, if my dirty mouth bothers, you have no one to blame but yourself." He lightly pinched the outside of her thigh, and she yelped at the slight sting.

"I never said it bothered me. I find it rather... stimulating."

"Do you now?" A devilish smirk emerged as he flattened his belly to the grass and draped her legs over his shoulders. "In that case, I won't hold back. Now, you're only allowed to say three words: more, please, Owen. Preferably in that order."

"But I... I..." An inkling of his intentions bubbled into existence, but she couldn't fathom him actually doing it. Did men do such things to their wives?

"Only those three," he repeated, then the only sounds emanating from him were deep growls and murmurs of delight as his tongue burrowed between her thighs to lick along her... pussy.

That's what he'd called it.

The wickedness of such a word aroused her, and she was eager to learn more from him. A lazy flick at her clitoris sent her back arching from the spongy ground and a gasp for air falling from her lips.

"That's it, love. Tell me what you like. I want to hear every pretty cry. Feel every tight squeeze of your sweet pussy on my tongue."

"Please, Owen... more." The requested command tumbled easily from her, and he acquiesced with a bruising grip on her hips. This version of the Owen she knew commanded easily, moved with confidence—versus the youth who'd been more hesitant, careful in his touches. *Though we never crossed this line before where his mouth devoured me like I'm one of his favorite treats.*

"Happy to oblige, wife. I'm glad you're taking your vow of obedience to heart." Teeth nibbled, lips sucked, as Owen's mouth took full advantage of his position, laying waste to any layer of resistance she may have held onto. She didn't want to rebuff him. Didn't want to hold him at a distance any longer.

She wanted what she always had, even when she'd denied it—Owen, plain and simple, the love of her life.

Two fingers entered her, working in tandem with the laving of his tongue. *Push, pull, push pull.* The rhythm increased as her whimpers grew louder. She'd attempted to replicate this feeling once. Tried to touch herself and imagine Owen's rougher hands.

It hadn't felt half as good—not because her smaller fingers couldn't reach as deeply as his or because she didn't give it her best shot—but because Owen's touch set her afire. The special effect belonged to him alone; it wasn't something she could conjure out of thin air.

His fingers changed angles until he pressed against something inside that drew a hoarse shout. "Owen, please... Don't stop..."

Taking his vow of obedience seriously, too, Owen focused all of his attention on her sensitive sex, until finally, with one surprising nip of his teeth, she came against his mouth, crying out from the sparks of pleasure bursting in every nerve ending.

Like the fireworks launched at the end of the fair—only brighter—singeing each exposed part of her at close range.

Shuddering from residual shockwaves, Lily expected him to remove himself after the last wave abated. Instead, he shifted her legs so his head rested on her left thigh, allowing his tongue to languidly stroke her at his leisure.

"You don't have to continue... I... um... finished." Never in her life would she have imagined voicing those words, but she didn't know how to handle Owen's absorption with her pussy. God, she felt naughty even thinking that word.

"Mmm... But I haven't." His hot breath brushed over her in the warmest of touches. "Just rest, darling. Let me have this. Love you the way I want to."

Oh, no.

Another crop of tears threatened to well over at his plea. She didn't deserve this man. She'd had the right of it earlier—he was too good.

Nevertheless, Lily didn't push him away, accepting what he wanted to give as this time he kept his movements featherlight and teasing, until a gentler orgasm surprised her, its lingering effects stronger than she would've expected.

Too good, indeed.

Struggling for breath, she lay redolent on the bank of the lake, grateful for the cloud drifting to block the sun for a moment. "Did you learn that on your travels as well?" She meant it as a teasing compliment, but feared it may have come out snarkier than she would've preferred. Owen's past liaisons weren't any of her concern, besides he'd claimed to be a virgin, perhaps that extended to all types of love play.

"No, I just happen to be a quick learner when my wife is exceedingly sensitive and vocal about her delight." His head lifted higher to rest just below her chest—the perfect temptation with his auburn hair drying in thick waves, begging for attention. Relaxing under his calm tone, no offense taken by her query it seemed, she dropped her hand to his temple and began stroking through the familiar strands.

She allowed her head to drift to the side where her gaze caught on the old oak tree across from them. The secret hiding spot for their letters to each other. Something she knew Owen hadn't used in years, except for the one demanding letter about meeting after their terrible coupling at his mother's ball.

Lily, however...

I should tell him. It's time.

CHAPTER SIXTEEN

Will you ever read these? Am I only writing in the wind, words carried to a far off place, never to be seen, to be understood by you? A true test of my bravery, I suppose.

"THERE'S SOMETHING I must show you." Lily combed delicate fingers through his hair while his head rested alongside her left breast.

"Hmm..." he murmured, relishing the touch of her hand and the sweet taste of her pleasure which lingered on his tongue. He'd never done that before. He'd heard of it. Seen it once. But he'd never cared to perform the intimate act for a woman if she wasn't Lily. Pride at his successful attempt swelled in his chest, and he palmed another turgid part of his body—the thick erection yearning for freedom. "Can't it wait? I'm quite enjoying this."

The taste of her had overwhelmed him to the point where all he wanted was to drown in her essence. To sip from her cup until he became drunk off her sweetness. And once she rested some more, he planned on continuing to quench his thirst, lazing by the lake for however long it took.

Even if my cock turns blue from denial.

Lily was the only one who mattered to him at the moment.

Her previously languid body tensed beneath him before gradually relaxing again. He wondered what could be so important that she'd need to show him right this second, but she acquiesced to his request, and he let the topic drop. "I suppose so. It is rather nice out... We can stop there on our way home."

"I was referring to enjoying more than the weather, Lily-pad."

She hummed in amusement. "I know. That was also *nice*."

Now, she was toying with him, but he didn't mind this playful side of her—in fact, he adored it. "Woman, if you think to goad me into proving my extreme prowess at licking your pussy by suggesting the first and second times you came on my tongue were merely nice... Well, consider myself properly provoked." Owen nuzzled the tender skin of her inner thigh before adding another love bite to match its twin on her other thigh.

"Wait, what about you?" Lily pushed on his head until he could see the determined set to her pretty mouth and the curiosity glowing in her golden eyes. *Hmm, it appears anger isn't the only emotion to elicit a change of color*, he mused.

"What about me?"

"Don't pretend ignorance. I want to please you, too. It's only fair."

Owen frowned in an expression of mock disappointment. "Lovemaking isn't about fair. We're not keeping tally of this or that to maintain a balance. We give and take as necessary out of l..." He almost said *love* but knew it would be a stretch at this point for her. Possibly for him, too. *Liar*. Clearing his throat, he changed course and said, "Out of care for the other. My turn can come later."

Proud of his quick thinking, he smirked as another reason for pride occurred to him. A medal bestowed upon him for his restraint wouldn't be remiss.

Though, his reasonings weren't altogether gallant. Yes, he wanted to satisfy Lily, focus on her pleasure alone. However, part of that need came from a fear of his own stamina. He'd never had a woman's mouth around his cock, and even the idea of Lily's pretty mouth wrapping around him...

Well, sad to say, Owen wasn't entirely sure he wouldn't spend the moment her lips brushed his skin.

Lily huffed in feigned annoyance before widening her legs in encouragement, reminding him of the task at hand—or rather, the nirvana before his mouth. "As you wish, dear husband. But don't be surprised when your turn might come sooner rather than later."

"Surprise won't be my chief emotion, I assure you," he muttered before diving in for a third helping of his wife's delicious pussy. It's a shame they'd spent so many years estranged; he would've liked to wake up every morning to her sweet form molded against his, able to kiss her sleep-flushed skin on a downward path before ending with his head between her legs.

Breakfast in bed. A decadence expected to be taken by an earl, no doubt. He hid a mischievous smile in Lily's intimate curls, his mouth easily gliding through her plump lips to collect more of her honey.

"Darling, have you ever tasted yourself?"

An incredulous squeak erupted above him, and he knew she was scandalized. Who'd have thought the indomitable Lily Lennox nee Taylor still had it in her to be shocked?

"Of course not! How could you... Why I never..."

"Shame, because you taste divine. Here, take a sip, trust me. I won't tell anyone what a naughty countess you are." Owen slanted his mouth over hers, a tad sloppy with her wetness clinging to his mouth and cheeks, but she welcomed him anyway. And moaned.

Bloody hell.

She fucking *moaned*.

Their tongues tangled haphazardly, none of the finesse of earlier. Their passions diluted to its purest form of raw hunger. "Lily, tell me you want this. Say you want me. Not to finish anything," he rasped, referencing her strike that first night they fucked. "But to begin again. I need inside you, darling. Please, let me..."

So much for your restraint. But to hell with it! Desperation called for begging, and Owen Lennox was damned desperate.

"Yes." Lily braced her hands on his shoulders and lifted her hips to nudge his cloth-covered cock. "Yes, make me yours, Owen. Finally."

Wrenching his cock free, he wasted no time lining himself up with her entrance before pausing. The specter of their last coupling reared its ugly head. *It's in the past. Expunge the memory with this. The perfect afternoon spent in your wife's embrace.*

"Owen?" Doubt crept over Lily's delicate features, and he hated being the reason to dim the light of joy brightening them mere seconds ago.

Smoothing a kiss over her brow, he whispered, "I want to make this perfect for us."

"It doesn't have to be," she returned, massaging the tense muscles at his neck and shoulders. "Besides, it can't be any worse than my initiation of our first time. I set a fairly low bar, nowhere near perfection."

He chuckled in disbelief, impressed they could joke about it now. "When you put it like that..." His playful tone faded as he stared down at her. She was so precious to him.

Patience worn thin, Lily's nails dug into his muscle as she urged him closer. "Owen, I swear everything will be fine. We both want this, and if it's not great, then we'll try again. You forget we're married and not teenagers rushing to clandestine rendezvouses. We've got time now to do this properly."

"You make too much sense for a woman supposed to be wild with lust for me and my cock."

"Then you and your cock better get to... What did you call it? Oh yes, *fucking* me senseless."

The crass demand spoken in her dulcet tones snapped the last of his hesitancy, and he thrust forward, fully to the hilt. His inexperience shot up like a damned weed, but he prayed he could retain a modicum of dignity.

Don't release within seconds of feeling her tight walls wrapped around your cock and call it a victory.

Strategy set, Owen inhaled a long breath, focusing on the expansion of his lungs—ignoring the thunderous thrashing of his heart—then forcing the air back out in a controlled exhale—not thinking about the persistent clenching of Lily's pussy.

Good god, this was the most wonderful... Torturous... Exhilarating... Embarrassing moment of his life. Any discipline he'd learned during their youth dissolved after seven years of disuse because his body stood on the precipice of release too *bloody* soon.

She said it didn't have to be perfect. Logically, he knew it to be true. However, male pride was another thing. *At least you've surpassed the length of that first time.*

Straining every muscle as he held himself still above her, Owen asked, "Are you alright? Should I wait longer before—"

"Owen..." she groaned in frustration—not the good kind—and he let himself go. Spending like a greenling? It may happen. Satisfying his wife beforehand? Still possible.

His hips slanted over hers, plunging deep in even strokes, his ballocks slapping against her arse, and the irrepressible swelling at the base of his cock signaled his oncoming release. Rolling to his back, he brought Lily around to straddle him.

"What... What are you doing?" Her words may have stuttered but her rocking body didn't. Despite the uncertainty in her mind, her body instinctively understood what to do.

"I need my hands free for this next part." Because he needed her to come. Now. While he maintained a thread of self-possession. One hand lowered to the point of their joining, a slower pace with Lily taking lead, and searched until he found the firm bud of her clit. Scissoring two fingers alongside the sensitive bundle of nerves, an immediate reaction came from Lily—the sweetest cry of amazement as she worked harder against him.

"That's it, sweetheart. Don't you prefer this? Fucking your husband with abandon. Riding me in full view of any passersby while I rub and suckle every inch of you I can reach?" To make good on his promise, Owen lifted to an elbow and caught a bouncing nipple in his mouth, drawing the pink bud between his teeth.

A thought towards gentleness passed through him, but Lily didn't seem to be in pain. To the contrary, she pressed herself further into him, urging him on. "More... Please, Owen... I need it harder."

Every cell concentrated on bringing her over the edge of orgasm with him. Bucking up into her slick pussy with harsh strokes—groaning at the explicit sounds of sex emanating from them. Pinching and rolling her clit between his fingers. Suckling roughly at her breast until the most exquisite taste leaked into mouth.

What the fuck?

They both paused for a split-second, shock written on both of their lust-crazed faces as the illicit desire he'd voiced earlier materialized, before resuming at a frantic race to the finish. Owen kept firm pressure on her breast and enjoyed more evidence of her pregnancy. *This is depraved.* Drinking his wife's milk—the sustenance meant for their babe. But the baby wasn't due for months, and opposition from Lily remained nonexistent.

And Lily said I could do whatever I please with her.

So, he took what he wanted and growled as the sweetest fucking cream he'd ever had ran down his throat.

"Don't stop..." Lily tightened around him. "Merciful heavens, why does that feel so good?"

"Because you're a naughty minx, wife, and a wild streak runs through you a mile wide." He switched to her other breast, and finally—*finally*—they could hold themselves together no longer.

Mutual shouts of satisfaction rose in the air as Lily's pussy clamped down on his cock, milking his seed from him in continual waves until she collapsed on his chest, their bodies slick and sticky with sex and sweat.

"Perhaps it's wise we waited so long to officially consummate our relationship. If we'd done that seven years ago, we're liable to have been caught and cast out with as much ruckus as we made."

Lily laughed, a joyful noise that resonated in his heart. *I fucking love her laugh.* "Can you imagine someone discovering us? It would've put my original scandal to shame."

"It could've put someone in the grave. If old Mr. Langston happened upon us, his poor heart may have given out." She smacked his chest in reprisal, but a chuckle of agreement bubbled forth, nonetheless.

"You shouldn't joke about such things. Fate has a way of doling out cruel fortunes."

Owen tipped her chin up. "I thought we were past this fight with fate? That's what this whole afternoon was about."

"Not the entire afternoon, thankfully." Lily yawned and nuzzled into his chest, allowing the topic to float away on the summer breeze cooling them down. "Shall we nap before heading home? All this exertion has tired me and the baby."

"You're not too sore or anything, are you? I know I was rougher than—"

"You were perfect. Including the bit where you drank from my..." She stopped short, burying her head as if to escape his heated gaze. "Well, it was all perfect, despite your worries. But I am tired, so if I've satisfied your concern over my well-being..."

"Quite, my lady. Feel free to nap to your heart's content." And he would lay here basking in her warmth, staying safe in the bubble they'd created—devoid of any of the troubles plaguing them outside.

ON THEIR TREK HOME an hour later, something weighed on Lily's mind, and he hoped it wasn't regret over their earlier tryst. Had he been overzealous?

Or perhaps she feels the weight of reality becoming heavier and heavier the closer we get to home. Owen hoped things wouldn't go back to the way they were, but every forward step with his wife seemed to precede three steps back.

"If you nibble any harder on that lip, it'll be bruised for a week. What's the matter, Lily-pad?"

"I'm scared I won't be a good mother. You're the good one, not me." The unexpected statement spilled forth like a dam finally breaking loose. And as far away from his guesses as could be.

"What makes you think that?" he asked carefully, avoiding any tone of accusation.

"At eighteen, I set out to seduce a man to end the affair with my noble lover."

Owen harrumphed at the dramatic retelling of their history, thankful that it didn't bear the intense pain it did even that morning when he saw her and Lynch. Perhaps their lake escapade had helped him release negative emotions as well.

Yes, except for the dull throbbing near your heart, he thought ruefully.

Attempting humor, he asked, "Have you spoken to Hazel lately, darling? There's been quite an embellishment to our story. A kiss with the stable boy hardly qualifies as a seduction." He almost choked on the last word, hating the knowledge that her solution to their perceived problem was betraying him with another man.

But you're forgiving her for the misjudgment, aren't you?

Stroking the side of her face with a tenderness borne of compassion, he continued, "Besides, we grew up in relatively happy families. A child of ours can't do worse than a family full of interesting aunts and a doting grandmother. Forget the silly notion of your bad luck or bad blood or whatever you want to call it. We dealt with that at the lake, and it's settled. There's nothing wrong with you, and you'll be a wonderful mother."

Lily cupped the back of his hand before stepping away, dodging broken branches and tangles of weeds as they followed the path through the forest home. "I lied to you, Owen. When you asked me how I felt about being pregnant, I said that I felt like other mothers. But that's not true."

She held a low hanging bough aloft for him to pass by her. "When Cara suggested I might be with child, my first thought was that I'm not ready. I didn't want this. Fate was punishing me again."

"And you still feel this way," he ventured, not so much a question as a confirmation.

"I don't know. Although we mentioned children briefly when we were younger, I never truly felt an urge towards motherhood. It was more a notion of pleasing you and doing what's expected." She paused, circling her extended belly with an expression of bafflement. One he wouldn't be surprised to learn he wore as well.

He thought every woman wanted to become a mother. Never in his wildest imaginings would he have considered otherwise.

"These past months, I've grown fonder of the idea, especially after seeing Zinnia's kittens. But my temperament doesn't seem fit for mothering. I'm not patient. I'll be short with the baby, despite knowing they can't help their crying or fits. What kind of mother is that?"

"We each have our flaws, love." He let the endearment slip out. "We'll learn together, and it's not like we'll be alone. We'll have help."

"They'll like my sisters better than me," she whispered dejectedly.

"No, sweetheart, that's not true." Owen's arms wrapped around her waist, overlaying her smaller hands. "Our child will love you."

Like I do.

Bending his head to the crook between her neck and shoulder, he kissed the elegant spot and wondered how it could be true.

He loved her, but a part of him struggled to completely trust her when it came to his heart.

A warring paradox raging inside him.

"Now, you know all of my secrets." A watery chuckle vibrated between them, only to be cut off by a groan of frustration. "Except that's not true. I forgot to show you what

I wanted to earlier." She playfully pushed him. "Thanks to your indecent behavior. We'll have to turn back."

"You want to go back now? Surely, it's not important enough to warrant a trip when we're this close to home."

Lily ignored him as he blocked her walk back to the lake. "Yes, it is. To pass the time, you can tell me a secret, so we're even. So I don't feel so strange and alone."

Taking her hand in his, he let her lead while debating what to share as their feet crunched along brittle leaves and sticks, retracing their steps. The two ominous scrolls he'd received came to mind, but he dismissed it. Lily didn't need to feel like their marriage was causing him more trouble than she already imagined.

Recalling another eventful moment on their wedding day, he relayed the revelation of Iris's possible biological father.

"The Marquess of Linton! Iris's sire?" Disbelief rang in the humid air, similar to his reaction to the news. "How is this possible? After all this time? What do you think he has to gain from announcing his parentage now?"

"I'm unsure. He claims only good intentions, but it does seem rather out of character from what I've heard about him."

"Why don't you hire an investigator to look into him like you did for Jonathan?" A flush rose to his cheeks as he twitched at the suggestion. Smirking, Lily explained, "Hazel told us about your chat with Jonathan. Can't you do the same with the Marquess? Once we have more information, I'd be more comfortable sharing with Iris."

It was a sound plan.

One I should've thought of despite all the upheaval lately.

Seemed like things kept slipping out of his grasp like sands in a time turner, and he wondered if some of Lily's beliefs about fate hadn't rubbed off on him. With things going wrong on the estate, the confusing scrolls, and the doubt he harbored about Lily's trustworthiness, perhaps his turn had arrived to be punished.

For defying his father's advice.

Nonsense!

Shaking his head of the dark musings, Owen responded with an affirmative—he'd notify a private investigator to learn more about the Marquess of Linton and his intentions towards Iris.

"Why is it the return journey seems so much quicker than the trek home?" The rhetorical question hung in the air as Lily brought them to their old hiding spot for notes. Reaching inside the tree hollow, she removed the familiar metal jewelry box he'd long-ago stolen from his mother's vanity—the once gleaming silver dull from years of weathering the changing seasons. Owen's eyes widened when Lily revealed the inside of the container, a pile of folded letters springing forth.

"What's all this?" Had she been writing to him all this time? For how long? He hadn't even thought to check this spot with all the animosity that had been between them, especially after his single note after the ball had gone ignored.

Owen kicked himself for the oversight.

"I wrote these as a way to release my feelings—my inner most thoughts—things I wouldn't let myself admit in the light of day. Emotions I fought until I lost and poured it out on the page so I could fight another day." Lily handed the thick sheaf of notes to him abashedly.

A filmy haze formed over her eyes as she met his, the sight of her vulnerability breaking his heart. "When I broke us, I think I inadvertently broke something inside myself, too. And, at times, I blamed you for the damage because you left. You believed Asa's lies. You didn't fight for me despite everything saying the contrary. Illogical really." She sniffled and shrugged. "Yet the broken hurt part of me wasn't capable of reason. You should have these now that we're on better terms. Now that we're moving forward together. Perhaps you won't judge my past actions so harshly with the knowledge of my true feelings in your hands."

"Lily..."

She raised a hand to stop him. "No, don't speak yet. Just read them. I'll wait for you in the stables with the kittens if you still want to talk." With a lingering glance of fondness, Lily cupped his cheek gently before turning away, leaving him to unravel the makeshift diary his wife had gifted him.

CHAPTER SEVENTEEN

The stables came into view, wood planks shining in the late afternoon sun, and Owen hurried to find his wife. He'd blazed through her letters, each more heartrending than the last until he finished reading all of them.

Our lips touched for the first time in years.

His Lily hid a soft heart. He'd always known it, but he'd forgotten—blinded by her harsh outward demeanor or devil-may-care attitude.

I'll leave you with a kiss until we're together again.

Her words rang in his mind on a loop.

Entering the cooler interior, the kittens were more awake this time around and hobbled over Lily's lap as she rested next to the feline family. Soon their child would join her—a child he knew she'd love with all her heart despite her misgivings about motherhood.

Sitting on the other side of Zinnia, he said, "I read every single one of your letters. Thank you for sharing them with me." There was more he could share, how they made him feel, but he could tell by Lily's expression that any more vocal acknowledgment would discomfit her. *My stoic little Lily-pad.* "I've named this one Rascal." Owen bent down to grab a black and white kitten in his palms, the baby trying to suck on his thumb.

"Fitting." Lily brought the two remaining kittens to her cheeks and smiled, relief at the turn of topic permeating her relaxed shoulders. "These are Homer and Shelley."

Confusion swept over his features, nose wrinkling. "A Greek poet and English novelist? Why?"

"The Iliad was Papa's favorite thing to read outside of biology journals, and Mama loved Frankenstein."

"How peculiar... What's your favorite book?"

"Don't you remember?" she teased, lowering the kittens to their mama, who lounged gracefully, tail twitching in the air. Memories descended of years prior, lively debates and playful arguments, until he remembered with a snap of his finger, which startled poor Rascal.

Returning him to his siblings, Owen grinned. "Gulliver's Travels! I remember now."

Standing tall, he brushed at the hay clinging to his trousers and lifted his chin to an obscenely superior angle. Affecting a nasally tone, he quoted, "Horrible, shameful, blasphemous!"

"Filthy in word, filthy in thought!" Lily finished, moving to her knees. They remained silent for a moment—recalling the insult from fellow novelist William Makepeace Thackeray about the book—before doubling over in peals of laughter. "When we discovered that review, we knew we'd found our favorite tale."

"To be sure. How could we resist something so dissolute?" Placing a hand over his racing heart, Owen allowed another rumble of amusement.

"Especially considering our own rather wicked natures..." The air shifted around them, imbued with an unexpected tension, as the delight in Lily's eyes transformed into something darker, desirous.

Owen looked down at his pregnant wife on her knees for him, and lust slammed into his gut at the implication of her position. *What implication? She's an innocent; she can't know such things.*

Not to mention you made love but a brief two hours ago.

Yet, her actions destroyed the thought immediately as she shuffled closer, hands landing on his hips, mouth level with his growing erection.

"What are you doing?"

"Something I've been curious about for years, and I did warn you that I would have my way with you sooner rather than later... Welcome to sooner." He wanted to kiss the cheeky grin off her lips but remained still, curious about her intentions. Nimble fingers unbuttoned his trousers, and his breath shook in his lungs. "I caught a maid and a footman behind your conservatory once. Her head bobbing up and down. His hand urging her forward. They both seemed to enjoy the act immensely with loud grunts and groans of satisfaction." A salacious grin winked up at him. "I want to make *you* groan in satisfaction. It's only fair after the pleasure you have already given me."

Bloody hell.

"Are you certain you wish to proceed? It's not necessary."

"On the contrary, dear husband, it's of the utmost importance to me."

Adam's apple bobbing, he nodded for her to continue. "If you must." Owen pretended to have control over his whirling emotions, over the desire running rampant through his blood.

He must make this good for her. Make it last as long as she wanted to please him this way.

Clear as crystal apparently, Lily chuckled at his forced forbearance. "Yes, dear husband. You must." Drawing him out of his loosened trousers, she studied the thick stalk before tracing a delicate fingertip down a particularly throbbing vein. "Not quite like the statues at the Museum of Art, hmm?"

He chose to take the question as a compliment, recognizing he was rather more endowed than the marbled men he'd witnessed in his travels. "Intimidated, sweetheart?"

"Is that a challenge, my lord? Because you know how I can't resist claiming a victory over you."

"Hard to forget when you remind me at every turn."

Her eyes rolled heavenward before she returned to her task of pleasuring him by flattening the pink tip of her tongue against the mushroom head of his cock. She didn't immediately lick or suck, only waited, and the anticipation brought forth a few drops of pre-cum that she quickly swiped into her mouth as if it was exactly what she'd wanted.

The minx. Where on earth did she learn that?

"You said the maid enjoyed this?"

"She made a little humming noise in her throat denoting pleasure." Then Lily mimicked the addicting sound by sucking him into her mouth. Tight muscles worked against him as he hit the back of her throat, and she reared back at the contact before attempting to try again.

God, bless her.

And him.

An errant thought flitted through his consciousness. It was fitting they should do this here, as if exorcizing the past demons of their lives. These stables had witnessed momentous occasions in their relationship—from its shattering to its mending. And this memory would be another brick in the foundation they were rebuilding together.

She drew a rough growl from him as her elegant fingers stroked in tandem with her pretty mouth, every once in a while dropping lower to cup his stones and roll them in her palms.

"Christ! Lily..." His hands stole into her disheveled braid. Unkempt after their lovemaking at the lake. The tangled strands wound around his fingers as his hips thrust into her, a lack of control coming over him. "Darling, you're doing so well. Do you like sucking my cock? Like feeling it fuck between your pretty red lips?"

An unintelligible murmur drifted up as her fervor heightened. Cheeks hollowed. Lips swollen. A wildness rampant in her golden gaze.

He was going to come. Spill his seed in his pregnant little wife's glorious mouth.

He thought to warn her. A gentleman surely would. But proper protocol escaped him as his cock spasmed, his hot release boiling over while Lily accepted with eagerness. Swallowing his seed and creating the lewdest sounds he'd ever heard, despite visiting every bordello in Italy with Brandon.

Sweet licks tenderly lapped at his semi-deflated cock—cleaning him in a manner so caring and wifely, a direct opposition to the aftercare of prostitutes he'd seen—that he felt his heart squeeze in response.

"Along with your language, you brought back voyeuristic tendencies, as well." The raspy tone of Lily's voice revived another spark of lust, its seductive nature luring him in like a siren's song.

"It's because of all the hiding we used to do."

Her ensuing snicker made him hopeful of a time when they would no longer hide from each other.

It'll come. Complete trust will bloom again.

Lily laid a string of kisses across his pelvis, sneaking underneath his shirt to brush his abdomen before returning him to his trousers and stumbling to her feet. He caught her arms in his hands and drew her in for a hug of gratitude. While not the most salacious of holds, his arms wrapped around her expanding waist and hers circling his shoulders held its own power of contentment. It settled his mind and heart with its simplicity.

"Perhaps, you're right," his wife murmured, resting her cheek on his chest. "Though, there's something to be said for voyeurism, I suppose. If I'd never caught that maid, then I never would've imagined taking you in my mouth, and what a tragedy that would've been because I quite enjoyed the experience."

Laughter burst from Owen and startled the cats, the horses, probably even the birds in the rafters, and he couldn't give a damn.

The Earl of Trent was reveling in his wife's candid banter, adoring her brazen ways.

CHAPTER EIGHTEEN

Days later, the unexpected sight of Owen napping at his desk greeted Lily as she entered his study. His head lay at an awkward angle to the side with Zinnia and Rascal cradled in his arms, one hand resting protectively over them while the other cupped Zinnia's fluffy tri-colored head. Contented purrs emanated from the pair of felines while Owen released slight snores upon every slow inhalation.

Retreating for a moment before inching forward on slippered feet, Lily lifted the folded quilt she'd stolen from the room next door to drape the patchwork blanket over her sleeping husband, careful not to disturb his or the cats' slumber.

Owen looked younger in such a peaceful state—the resemblance to the auburn-haired boy of her past tugging forth memories she no longer tried to keep buried. A feeling of lightness trailed her steps these days after talking with Owen. After spewing forth every dark thought and secret she harbored like a lanced wound.

A seven-year-old wound.

A lock of hair tickled his brow, and Lily's hand trembled. It would be so easy to brush it aside, and there was no reason to keep her distance anymore. Temptation teased, urging her to touch him—gently, intimately.

Why are you resisting? You've both chosen to move forward.

"Dash it all," she muttered, a tentative hand smoothing the wayward tendrils.

This was her husband, the love of her life. The father of her child. A man who treated her kindly despite her brash attitude and past mistakes.

And she could admit to herself finally that perhaps fate hadn't been as malevolent as she'd assumed by forcing their hands, by bringing them back together.

Owen's words at the lake reverberated in her mind.

She had been viewing life with an eye towards failures and bad outcomes, ignoring the very real positives that filled her days now. It was time to let go of the past and look towards the future. One where they were happy and in love.

Of course, neither of them had shared those words, yet.

But for the first time in years, she felt hopeful. Her heart already beat for him entirely. She needed only to wait for the appropriate moment to reveal the truth to Owen, a moment where he'd reciprocate the sentiment. Her letters had called him her love, of course, but she'd never outright written the three important words, let alone voiced them.

Turning to leave the napping trio, her eye caught on a crumpled sheet of paper on the carpet, a black ribbon beside it.

Strange.

Your wife humiliates you with another man. Have you no respect for your father's wishes?

Glancing at Owen, still peaceful in repose, Lily reread the note, a glacial frost rising to encompass her entire being. An ominous yawning of the black pit in her stomach. The letter dropped from her frozen fingers.

Who would write such a thing?

Two more wrinkled missives rested on the desk, and carefully leaning forward, she read the scrawled lines with a sinking dread.

She hadn't been wrong. She was no good for Owen.

The fact that someone felt compelled to send him these vile notes confirmed it. Proved that she only brought him trouble. Would've earned his father's disapproval.

And he chose to hide it from her.

All too easily her previous doubts burst forth for dominance—the sliver of solace inside banished like it never existed.

Lily looked down at the swell of her belly. Tiny and vulnerable, a fragile being residing inside her. Her hand involuntarily moved forward to brush the bump before jerking back, ashamed.

"I'm sorry."

She apologized for not being good enough, for causing the child's father such heartache. "You don't deserve this." Holding back tears, Lily left the study and headed outside, where a storm began to rage.

"My lady!" One of the maids called out. "My lady, where are you going? It's about to storm terribly out there!"

But Lily ignored the concern and continued her trek outside. Deafening chastisements bombarded her, ringing in her head—blocking out all other voices.

CHAPTER NINETEEN

"Owen, have you seen—"

The genteel voice of his mother woke him from a pleasant dream of Lily and him in the gazebo enjoying a picnic. *I'll have to make that a reality.* Zinnia and Rascal's claws dug into him at being disturbed, before they hopped onto his desk, curling up in the corner by a lamp.

"Oh, I apologize, dear. I didn't think you'd be sleeping at this hour." Gliding forward, she adjusted her skirts before taking a seat and caressing a hand over Zinnia's fur. "I was looking for Lily and thought you might know where she's gotten off to."

"No, I haven't a clue." He patted his cheek in an effort to eradicate the lingering vestiges of sleep. An afternoon nap hadn't been on the agenda, but after receiving another mysterious note with no clue as to its sender, a headache had formed. And he'd allowed himself to doze off in order to forget—for a moment, at least—his problems.

Sinister messages. Various estate accidents.

It occurred to him that they might be connected, but for what purpose, he couldn't decipher. Searching for the tossed sheet of this last message, a frown tugged at his lips. *Where the devil is it?* He crushed it in his fist. Thrown it to the floor. But it was nowhere to be found.

"Hmm... perhaps I'll ask a maid." Rising to her feet, she turned to leave before noticing her son's peculiar behavior. "Have you lost something, dear?"

"Just a letter."

"None of those are the one you seek?" She gestured to three pieces of parchment on his desk, and he stilled at the appearance of the one he sought.

"Yes, actually, it is." Jumping to his feet, he hurried to the hall. "If you'll excuse me, I think I might need to speak with Lily first." There wasn't a clue to suggest Lily moved the paper, but a feeling of dread slithered down his spine.

She imagined fate held a vendetta against her.

She'd guessed at his father's feelings toward her.

Now, his wife had seen proof in the letters that there was indeed some trouble brewing due to their union. What she'd do with the knowledge was anyone's guess. But based on what he knew of her past decisions, it couldn't be good.

Catching a dawdling maid in a blue sitting room, he asked, "Have you seen my wife?"

"Oh, yes, my lord. I tried to warn her, but she didn't listen—"

Apprehension locked around his shoulders. "Where is she? What happened?"

"She raced outside like the hounds of hell were at her heels, my lord. And with it kicking up a storm out there."

"And you didn't think to notify me or another member of staff to go after her?" Rain smacked against the windowpane in a rush of power while thunder echoed overhead. And his pregnant wife was somewhere in it, unprotected.

Leaving the gaping girl a stuttering mess, Owen ran past his mother who'd followed him to see what the fuss was about, and sprinted through the front doors to Marvin's consternation.

"My lord!"

The words whipped away as quickly as they were uttered. Coatless and already soaked to the bone, Owen prayed to find Lily on her way back home as he headed toward the one place he knew she'd go—the lake.

CROWS' CAWING PIERCED the sound of bending branches in the windswept forest—a prophetic backdrop considering her mood. It spoke of haunted woods and witches' curses and ghostly apparitions. All things she ordinarily wouldn't give two figs about except the idea that some supernatural force could be the cause of all her misfortune didn't seem too outlandish anymore.

Was she destined to live a life marred by tragedy?

An unlucky traveler on the road of life?

A particularly gusty breeze whipped against a tree to her left, the snap of a gnarled branch preceding a crash to earth. It wasn't safe to walk this path. Not at this time. But she didn't dare return home.

Home.

A bitter laugh scraped against her vocal cords.

What was home? A husband who cared for her when she didn't deserve it, a man she only brought trouble upon.

And the baby within her—a poor child who'd be stuck with her as a mother—a terrible destiny.

The drum of rushing water rose above the howling wind as she neared the river, careful to keep a distance from its treacherous tides. She'd decided to take the roundabout path to the lake, passing Shoreham Bridge, instead, as a sort of punishment. Swelling past the embankment, the overflowing river was a marked contrast to the rocky bottom where her parents died a few years ago.

Head tilted back towards the sky, Lily released a strangled shout of despair. Emotions whirled inside her as if the storm outside had manifested inside her body. It wouldn't surprise her if a strike of lightning was drawn to her chaotic energy.

Suddenly, one of the branches overhead snapped under the force of the wind, crashing with deadly force towards the ground. Lily attempted to avoid the falling bough, but her slippered feet slid in the mud, and she tumbled down the steep embankment into the roaring waves of the river. Ice cold soaked through her dress and dragged her deeper into the dark abyss.

Lily remained still instead of fighting to the surface, wondering if this is how it was all supposed to end. Fate would drown her in the same river that killed her parents.

Chunks of debris brushed against her skin, and she accepted the little bites of pain. Isn't that what she'd always done? Accepted what life gave her, only letting the bitterness build and build until her life had come to this. A mortal struggle in the gnashing jaws of a storm-swept river.

No.

A pointed declaration, one that fought its way into her mind.

This is not how I end.

Not how my baby's life ends.

I am tired of taking and accepting what life throws at me as if I have no choice in the matter.

I get to choose. To fight back. I am not leaving Owen; I am not harming my child.

I am not leaving my family.

Determined energy swelled from deep inside as her legs began to kick strongly against the waves, arms waving haphazardly in the water as her lungs were about to burst in need of air. Breaking through the surface of the river, she heard a faint shout of relief and her name carried over the shrieking wind and roaring water.

"Lily! I'm here! Swim to the side!" Owen's words reached her as she caught a glimpse of him running along the river bank trying to catch up to her.

"Don't jump in!" she tried to yell, terrified that he would try to save her. If he jumped and perished... She couldn't bear the possibility. Her head dunked under the water, brackish water flooding her mouth as she prepared to warn him away again.

Fight, Lily. Fight.

Renewed strength filled her aching body—allowing her shaky limbs to kick and paddle—until she surged forward, her toes finding purchase in the slick muck below. Strong arms wrapped underneath hers and tugged her further away from the killer water. "Thank God, you made it."

Frantic hands roved her body, cupping her belly, her face.

"I love you, Owen." Lily choked out, afraid she'd lose her chance to tell him her true feelings out loud as strength quickly left her tired limbs. "And I love our child. I'm so sorry." Soon the dark overtook the last piece of her consciousness, and she fainted in his arms.

CHAPTER TWENTY

"Lily, wake up!" Owen pressed his cheek to her chest, reassured by the steady heartbeat, but fear knotted itself around his heart. She loved him. And he loved her. He regretted not sharing his feelings after reading her letters.

But while words like *love* and *adore* inundated her words, the fact that she'd never said them aloud had created doubts. *Stupid fool.*

She needed to wake up so he could tell her. She needed to live. "Sweetheart." Gently shaking her, praying for her to regain consciousness. "Please, don't leave me."

A coughing fit erupted from Lily, and he hurried to turn her on her side as she gasped for air. Torrential rain continued to drive into the ground with a vengeance, pelting them with its pointed stings.

"Sweetheart, speak to me. Are you injured?" He ran his hands along her shivering body. "We need to get you home and out of this storm."

A small moan accompanied the negative shake of her head. "I'm sore, but I don't think anything is damaged beyond repair. Unless the baby..." Another shudder wracked her body while terror gripped him.

"The baby's fine. Everything will be fine." He had to believe it to be true. "Let's get you somewhere warm. I may never let you walk the river alone again; I thought I lost you, love."

"I thought I lost me, too. But somehow I found myself instead."

The strange statement confused him, but there would be time enough for questions when they were back home safe and sound under dry blankets and a fire roaring in the fireplace. He'd have the doctor fetched, and all would be well. It had to be.

Wrapping an arm around her back and beneath her knees, Owen struggled to his feet in the slippery mud.

"Let me stand. I can walk."

"You've just survived almost drowning. I'm carrying you home until we're positive you're as healthy as a newborn colt."

"Did you just compare me to a horse?" His laughter of relief stopped short when a faintly familiar voice broke through the thundering storm.

"Glad to see the river didn't drown out your spirit, girl." Both of them searched the trees for its owner when a man stepped forward, pistol held aloft in his hands. His gait unsteady under the pummeling rain, he nevertheless managed to keep the weapon pointed in their general direction, and Owen noticed what appeared to be dark splotches marring his skin.

"Mr. Laramie? What are you doing out here?" Lily recovered from her shock first, shouting the question uppermost in their minds, and with a flash of insight, Owen knew.

"It's you. You're the one who's been sending those menacing letters. But why?"

"Isn't it obvious? You stole my bride from me. Which is why I've been watching, waiting for my opportunity to exact vengeance. Camping in the wilderness isn't new to me." Owen wondered how long the man had been squatting on their land. How much he'd seen. Laramie continued, "It seems the misfortune of my shelter falling victim to this storm worked in my favor, though, because in my search for a new campsite, who do I discover but my quarry weak and defenseless."

Turning to Lily, Laramie's eyes held a maniacal glint. "You would've been the perfect wife: suitable for traveling for my research, tending to my line of future heirs. Compromised, ruined, yet the conniving bitch managed to become a countess."

"So, you decided threatening me would be your revenge? To what end? How did you know about my father?"

Laramie shrugged. "It's common knowledge among certain people about the tainted legacy of your family lineage. It wasn't difficult to put two and two together. Except you didn't heed my warning. You didn't honor your father by bedding then discarding the girl. Instead, you kept her by your side."

Struggling for Owen to let her stand on her feet, Lily muttered under her breath. "No wonder you needed my father's help." Wrapping her arms around her middle protectively, in a louder voice she said, "The crux of my scandal was Owen and I's relationship. If you'd learned the truth, you might've known Owen would never abandon me, nor I, him."

"'Tis no matter to me now." One hand gestured to his face. "It seems I've not long to live, according to London's finest doctors. Skin cancer, they say, from all my travels in particularly sunny areas." He spat the words out. "Couldn't even conceive an heir in time to keep my name alive, thanks to you."

Ah, so there lay the crux of the matter. Owen figured seeing Lily swell with his child so soon, when it could've been Laramie's babe, didn't sit well with the dying man.

"So, the two of you formed a love match." Disgust coated Laramie's voice as he loomed nearer. "Perhaps you'll reunite in the afterlife." Laramie shrugged, gray hair matted to his cheeks, obscuring part of his face.

"I empathize with your situation. Truly. It appears even I wouldn't wish death on my worst enemy. But what motive do you have to murder us? Because you didn't get your way? Like a child?" Owen squeezed Lily, worried her taunting would push Laramie over the edge, though the man appeared fairly close on his own. He wondered how far the cancer had progressed. Perhaps to the man's mind; it would explain this convoluted vendetta.

"What can I say? I don't like losing." He raised the pistol towards Lily, and Owen shoved her behind him. "No one will ever guess I'm to blame for the tragic loss of the Earl of Trent and his Countess. I'll be on a ship bound for the Indies, as my final send-off, while your bodies are ravaged by the river. A fitting end in my mind."

"Not in mine." Owen lunged for the deranged man as a shot rang out, and he clutched his shoulder—a burning fire shooting down his arm.

"No!" Lily's piercing scream rose above the din, but he kept charging towards Laramie. The man had used his one shot, and to Owen's mind, he'd wasted it.

Owen lived.

But he'd make damn sure Laramie didn't.

※

EVERYTHING SEEMED TO happen at once. The storm. Her revelations. Almost drowning. Laramie. And now Owen shot.

Before today, she might've let despair overtake her. Might have chalked this up to the general course of her life. But she knew better now.

Careening to the side, she kept Owen and Laramie in sight, the two men struggling for dominance as she searched the tree line for a weapon. A bulky branch stuck out of the ground near a large oak—a hefty bludgeon, if she had her way. The wood slipped beneath her palms and small splinters broke off into her skin, but she ignored the discomfort, raising the limb overhead to rest on her shoulder. Bracing a hand against the trunk, Lily rested for a moment, lungs desperately gulping in mouthfuls of air, before heading towards the continuing battle near the river's edge.

Silver flashed in the air as Laramie pulled a knife from his boot after wriggling free of Owen. Haphazard lunges followed, forcing her husband to dip and dodge.

I need to help him. Dragging in one last fortifying breath, Lily yelled, "Owen, duck!" the second before she swung the branch with all her might like a cricket player driving for the game-winning hit—her husband's auburn head avoiding the oncoming blow. The collision with Laramie's shoulder sent a bone-rattling jolt through her arms while shoving their attacker to the ground, where Owen pounced like a leopard in wait.

Straddling the man's chest, punch after punch cracked against Laramie's cheeks and nose until blood mixed with the rain and mud—the knife falling from his loosened grip.

"Owen... Owen!" Lily dropped the makeshift bludgeon and fell to her knees, hugging Owen from behind. "Enough! It's over. You mustn't kill him."

"But he deserves it. He wanted to harm you and our unborn babe."

"I know, but we can't lose you. I don't want his death on your hands for the rest of our lives." She pointed at the marks on Laramie's skin. "He will suffer enough from his own body turning on him."

He paused, considering her words, and she felt his body relax into her. His sense of honor overcoming the need for revenge.

With Laramie unconscious, Owen climbed off the prone man, and Lily sighed in relief, rearing back enough to examine the wound at his shoulder. Clean through and through. Grateful for the stroke of good fortune, Lily tried to find a relatively clean spot of clothing to tear off to bind the wound temporarily.

"We look like mud people." The attempt at a joke brightened the tense moment marginally, as did the lightening of rain. "I can't wrap the bullet holes with these or else your risk of infection will increase."

"Then, I suppose you should hurry home to fetch help. I'll watch Laramie to make sure he stays put until a footman binds and carries him home for the constable to deal with."

Kissing his cheek, Lily repeated. "I love you."

"And I love you, darling. Now run along, and be careful of slick spots and weakened branches. That was one helluva storm."

"It's been one helluva day."

"That it has been, love. That is has."

CHAPTER TWENTY-ONE

As soon as Lily entered the foyer, dripping wet and shivering, the house became a hive of activity. Men were sent to find Owen and Laramie, while another man rode for the doctor.

And in the midst of all the chaos, the previous hours took their toll and Lily found herself crying in her mother-in-law's arms on the staircase.

"There, there, my dear. Everything will be alright. You and the baby will be pronounced healthy, and Owen's injury will be stitched up."

Another sob wracked her aching body. "How can you be so forgiving? This is all my fault! If I hadn't run off into a storm like a ninny, none of this would've happened."

"Nonsense. This Laramie fellow surely would've found another opportunity to attack, especially with the continuation of those letters. At least now, he's taken care of." Her logical assessment settled Lily somewhat, though she still felt like she deserved more of a scolding before forgiveness.

Shouting preceded the group of men who burst through the entryway. Laramie had woken from his slumber and was putting up quite the fight for his release.

"Take him to the drawing room while we wait for the constable. The rain seems to be letting up finally, so he should be here soon." Owen directed from his place at the back of the group. Sidling past the moving men, he rushed to Lily and his mother, falling to his knees to embrace them.

"Thank goodness, you made it back safely. How are you feeling? Any trouble with the baby?"

"Not yet. Still kicking like normal, which I take as a positive sign," she admitted, both of their hands stroking her stomach.

"A very good sign, dear." The dowager countess smiled at the tableau before her, relieved to see her son and his wife in decent health. "Owen, I've been told you were shot. Let's have a look before Dr. Pearson arrives."

They all shuffled upstairs to the master suite, where the doctor found them a half-hour later—Owen's shoulder gleaming white from a fresh bandage and Lily dressed in a nightgown under the blankets of their bed.

"Good evening, my lord and ladies. Everyone looks to be alive and well, I'm happy to report. Now, let's examine the patients."

Owen motioned for the man to check Lily first, and so the elderly man began.

It wasn't until hours later that Owen and Lily were left alone, gazing at the blazing fire warming the room.

"I'm glad you and the baby are doing well after today's events." Owen rubbed her bump from his position beside her on the bed, his good arm hugging her to him while his injured arm rested in a sling. His steady strength eased the tension in her back and gave her the courage to apologize for her actions precipitating their harrowing ordeal.

"Me, too... I'm sorry I ran off like I did, though." Squeezing his hand, she closed her eyes against the dim light, inhaling deeply. "I put myself and our child in danger instead of confronting you about those notes. I let my fear take control."

A resigned sigh ruffled her hair as he considered her admission. "I should have told you about them, but I was scared to heap more troubles at your feet considering what we were already dealing with, but it's no excuse." She clung tighter to his hand, knuckles whitening at the vulnerable confession. "Fear controlled me, too."

"We both need to grow and trust each other more. Though, I wouldn't have guessed Laramie's part in this either way. I probably would've guessed Asa." The old stableboy certainly hadn't liked her rebuff at the luncheon or Owen's consequential threats.

"Lynch did come to mind," Owen admitted. "But his motive never materialized, except to hurt us, which I suppose was motive enough. I'm just glad it's over, and we can move forward as we should." Nuzzling into her neck, his lips pressed a lingering kiss to the downy hairs tickling his cheeks. "From now on, I vow to love and trust you completely. The past is buried, and I choose this Lily—the woman in my arms—rather than allowing your youthful self to color our future."

"I love and trust you, too. Over negative thoughts and fears. Over fate's perceived vendetta against me. I'm ready to move on."

"I'm happy to hear that, wife, because I know the perfect way to proceed." A mischievous note entered his voice as his hip nudged hers. Delicate nibbles etched her skin before finding her ear. "We have yet to fully consummate our marriage bed."

A miracle when she considered how far their intimacies had gone. Yet, they'd always eased away before crossing the line at home, as if an invisible barrier lay between them.

Empty tree copses and lakeside trysts are apparently our preferred locations to make love. The notion amused her, though it didn't come as a surprise with their propensity for the outdoors.

"And you think now is the appropriate time?" she goaded him, arching into his touch.

"As long as you're well enough…" Owen wavered with concern, but she smiled and nodded, undulating against him.

"*Very well*, dear husband. And very eager."

A rumble of approval vibrated at her side, and his hands quickly smoothed over her leg to raise her nightgown, urging her to straddle him. "Since you're quite round at the front and I'm down one arm, I believe this might be an easier manner with which to fuck you, my dear."

Polite then filthy.

The switch shocked and aroused.

"Whatever you want. I'm at your disposal." *Always*.

Through awkward shuffling, they managed to rid her body of the nightgown, revealing her naked body to the glowing firelight as she sat in front of Owen, facing away from him. Lily shivered. Despite all their touches, she'd never been fully bare to him. Clothing always remained in place, if a bit mussed and loosened.

Your wet chemise at the lake in full sunshine didn't offer much protection, if you'll recall.

Nonetheless, vulnerability like she'd never felt before crept forward as self-consciousness stole her thoughts. What would Owen think of her body? Her round, *pregnant* body? It wasn't the lithe form of an eighteen-year-old or the fit body of their first time together. Would it matter to him?

It didn't at the lake. Hold on to that.

Hoisting a heavy breast in his palm, Owen tweaked a hardening nipple, making her gasp. "Don't worry," he whispered. "I remember how sensitive these are. How sensitive you are... everywhere."

Curling deeper into Lily so her entire body felt surrounded by him, Owen's hand lowered, skimming over her belly until he slipped between her thighs. He shifted one of her legs over, spreading her wider for his invasion, her knees digging into the mattress.

"Is this comfortable enough for you?"

"Yes, though I didn't realize we could do it this way."

"Darling, as long as my cock can sink into your pussy, we can do it however which way we want," he promised, summoning a clench of her thighs in response. That's what she wanted. To have him anyway she could. To leave no stone unturned as they explored each other, finally able to freely express their love.

Casting her head to the side, Lily searched for his lips until his mouth found hers while his fingers circled her clitoris. He swallowed her gasp of delight and kept a steady thrumming along the bundle of nerves. Undulating into the exquisite touch, she followed his rhythmic circling, lowering a hand to clutch him closer.

"I confess to impatience, love. I need you inside me. *Now*." They'd waited too long. Prolonged foreplay would have to wait for another time because she couldn't take the emptiness without him any longer. The memory of being atop him at the lake seared her mind. The thick impression of his cock swelling inside her. His tongue and teeth plying her nipples and eliciting her breastmilk—something she hadn't expected so soon before the baby's arrival, let alone something she'd find immensely pleasurable. "Make me yours. Please."

"Lily... As much as I want nothing more, I don't trust my control once your hot walls tighten around me. I can't guarantee your pleasure, except through this." He increased the friction of his fingers against her. "Rubbing this sweet pearl until you spend on my hand. Then I can take you, knowing you've at least found your release."

Always so considerate. It bedeviled her. It endeared her.

"I don't care, Owen. We have the rest of our lives to learn each other, to give each other pleasure. What I want at this moment is your cock filling me up. I need to feel you," she begged, uncaring of the whimper in her voice. She ached for his possession. "Please, Owen. More."

THE REMINDER OF THEIR tryst at the lake, the first time he ate her pussy, the first time they'd truly fucked, pushed him over the edge. She gave him the words he wanted to hear; he wouldn't refuse her plea, now. Couldn't if he tried.

Undoing his trousers, Owen angled his cock to her wet entrance, slipping between luscious thighs, her plump bottom cradling him. This view undid him. His wife astride his cock.

AN EARL LIKE ANY OTHER

Her back pressed to his chest, leaving her entire front exposed to his every whim—a tug on her nipple, a caress to her belly, a rough stroke against her clit.

"I love you, sweetheart." He solidified the declaration with a thrust of his hips, plunging his cock to the base in one harsh go. They both groaned at the contact, and he relished her enveloping heat, thankful he could stay as long he could last—which in truth would probably be woefully short at this point—but at least it was a direct contrast of their first joining. And hopefully a surpassing of their second.

"I love... you, too," Lily stuttered, breath hitching as her back arched. "Feel so full. You're so thick."

Bloody hell.

A man can't be expected to last when his woman voiced such things. Especially a former virgin with only two tups under his belt. *If he even counted that first time...*

"Are you trying to make this difficult for me, woman?"

"Difficult? No. You're the one who's being hard to handle."

He chuckled at her cheek and burrowed deeper in her pussy. Another satisfied moan wisped over his lips.

"Puns in bed? You're thinking too much, love." Twisting her torso towards him, Owen bent his head and latched onto a rosy nipple and suckled his sweet prize. He loved her breasts. He loved them before her pregnancy, and he adored them even more now.

Would adore them even more if they gave him another scandalous taste of their creamy bounty.

Aiming to earn his prize, Owen ravished the pale globe—nipping and kneading, worshiping Lily. The rhythmic pulsing of her pussy on his cock mimicked each pull of his mouth, and he knew he wouldn't last much longer. *Fucking embarrassing.* But he'd improve. He'd learn to control himself so well that he could fuck her for hours every night.

Suckle her breasts. Perhaps make her come from that alone.

Devour her pussy until the sheets lay rumpled and soaked beneath them, her slick glistening on her thighs and his face.

Then impale himself in her warmth and stay there. Perhaps see how long they could withstand the stillness. Just reveling in their intimate connection.

Yes, he'd learn restraint, and he'd enjoy every second of it.

A cry arose from Lily as the first drop of liquid gold coated his tongue, and his hips roughly bucked forward, his shaft forcing its way into her hotly flexing walls, eager to wring more of those breathy sounds from his wife. Owen flicked and prodded, milked and rubbed her engorged clitoris until he recognized the tremulous flutters signaling her release.

"That's it, sweetheart. Spend for me." Licking away a stray droplet, Owen's strokes became erratic as they flew into oblivion together, a shriek of pleasure piercing the air as his growl of satisfaction erupted. Silky warmth seeped between them, dampening the sheets, but they didn't notice, too entangled in each other.

"And you were afraid of displeasing me." Lily contracted around his semi-hard erection. "That doesn't seem possible when we're together." She extricated herself from his grasp after catching her breath, carefully climbing off to lay on her side and face him, her belly pressing into his hip.

"I underestimated my skills, apparently," he joked, unduly pleased by himself.

Lily's joyful laugh tickled his senses, and he joined her in amusement. His chest felt light. Like he could float away, content with his life in every way.

"You've no shame either. With an ego as big as—"

"My cock?" he supplied with a teasing grin.

"Oh dear, I'll never hear the end of this now." She brought the covers over her face to hide in mock indignation.

"Well, you did call it *thick*, and I believe you were quite *full*?"

Primly, she explained, "A lady isn't responsible for whatever spills forth while making love."

"Is that so?" He whipped the blankets back to reveal her blushing face and kissed his lovely wife. "What about declarations of love?"

"I don't recall voicing any declarations or hearing them, for that matter."

"My mistake, wife. It shall be rectified immediately because..." He skated a reverential hand over her cheek to bury in the skeins of tangled hair on the pillow. "I absolutely, unconditionally love and adore you. You are my argumentative, brash, bright, and beautiful wife. The lone woman able to challenge me and win... on occasion." Owen grazed his lips over her wrinkled nose, inwardly laughing at her reaction.

"I can always count on you to follow any complimentary assertion with one of daring," she said. "However, it's comforting knowing your steadfastness in character. You were my first love—my only love—and I vow to protect your heart better than I have in the past. You're the only person in the world who truly understands and accepts me, even more than my sisters, and I will cherish that gift for as long as I live." A blush bloomed on her skin at the sentimental admission. His Lily wasn't one for such extended verbal displays of emotion, at least softer emotions.

But she wouldn't be the woman he loved otherwise.

Her fingers traced the faint growth of his beard and leaned forward for another kiss. Conversation complete, they basked in their newfound intimacy, caressing skin, whispering hopes for the future.

The perfect start to their new beginning.

EPILOGUE ONE

FOUR MONTHS LATER

"NO, WAIT! I WANT MY sister." A panicked note entered Lily's voice, fear written in the tense lines marring her face. "Iris, stay... Please."

"I'm sorry, my lady, but we must insist that all non-essential persons leave immediately. Besides, it's not appropriate for an unmarried young lady to witness such an event." The doctor patted Lily's hand in a gesture of comfort, but she drew away as another contraction ripped through her body. "Mrs. Middleton and I are more than capable of—"

Owen interrupted from his post against the wall where he'd been relegated as soon as he'd arrived at the news of her labor. "Whatever my wife wants, she'll have, proprieties be damned." Vehement firmness brooked no argument, and a spark of gratitude filtered through Lily's pain at the authoritative change. Due to his usual friendly attitude, she sometimes forgot Owen could still bring down all of the lordly power that was his right.

"But my lord..."

"The Countess of Trent is currently having my heir, Dr. Pearson, and by the looks of it, her sister is doing more to ease her than you." Owen motioned pointedly to Iris, who was wiping Lily's sweaty brow with a cool wet rag. "If you value your position, you'll stop arguing with me and do your job."

Cowed by the command, the doctor bowed his head in acquiescence and dug around in his leather bag before removing a plethora of metal tools. The clanking steel rattled in Lily's ears, and images of sharp edges, gleaming points, and blood ratcheted the sickly fear pervading her veins to a higher, agitated state. A whimper of protest trembled in the air.

"I can't do this." Wild eyes darted to Owen as he knelt on the bedside opposite of Iris. "I can't. Owen, please..."

"My darling, Lily-pad, we will get through this." He raised one of her hands to his cheek, kissing the back before cradling it protectively. "You are the strongest, most determined person I know. You're afraid, and I am, too, but you're no coward. You're my brave countess who doesn't balk at challenges. Soon, this will be over, and we'll have our child, all because of your strength and courage."

"He's right," Iris said, dampening another rag and gently patting at her sister's forehead. "There's no need to worry. Everyone in this room is here to help you."

"But I can't be a mother. I'm not ready." Turning her head back towards Owen, she pleaded. "You know I'm not ready. Oh god..." Another contraction bent her almost in half, knocking the wind from her lungs.

How had women borne this pain for millennia? How had her own mother birthed two more daughters after Caraway?

Lily couldn't imagine a more primitive, body-breaking pain than the one tearing through her at this moment. The reward of a baby, a child she couldn't fathom in reality, simply was not enough.

"Pardon, my lady, but I must check to see how far along the babe is. Perhaps you'd wait outside, my lord?" Dr. Pearson motioned to the door, obvious consternation at the presence of not one but two interlopers during his exam written in the scrunch of his bushy eyebrows.

"No, I will not. I'm not leaving my wife."

Gratitude and pride pushed through the pain. She loved her husband. Loved his resolute loyalty and kindness.

"I suppose that goes for you, too, miss?" the man asked Iris, and she nodded, a steel gleam in her eyes. They were only missing Caraway, who was visiting Hazel and Jonathan in Manchester. However, Owen had sent a letter notifying them of her labor, so they should arrive on the train soon.

Three spirited sisters. A beautiful child. One loving husband.

The perfect family for her.

Something she never thought would happen after the mistakes she'd made—mistakes she still made. But with age and Owen's support, her bitterness had waned, her anger tempering to a low simmer that only sparked during particularly frustrating arguments. Otherwise, she'd learned to accept her emotions and whatever fate decided to toss in her path.

A supremely easier and happier way to live.

Focusing on the good things in her life, Lily huffed and puffed through labor, pushing through pain and tears. It almost felt like a rebirth for her as their baby came into the world, wailing at the top of his lungs.

A new beginning.

And as she slumped against sweat-soaked pillows, precious little son in her arms and Owen holding them both in awe, Lily breathed in deep and exhaled the last vestiges of her old life.

EPILOGUE TWO

TEN YEARS LATER

"BENJAMIN JAMES LENNOX! Give that back right this instant!" A little girl with red pigtails stomped her feet as she stared up into the tall oak tree where Owen's son sat grinning like a fool.

"Just like his father, I see." Lily smirked, her arm weaved with his. They continued to approach the children with their littlest one in tow—Miss Edwina Lennox.

"Papa, I want to climb a tree, too."

"When you're older, poppet." He hoisted his daughter higher on his hip and basked in the warmth of his family's presence. After Laramie's demise all those years ago, the estate righted itself, running smoothly again, and allowing him to realize he was doing as well as his father would expect. Peaks and valleys were a constant in life, and he'd been a fool to think otherwise. To think his marriage to Lily affected it negatively.

"Ben, why are you torturing poor Miss Helen?" he asked from underneath the boy. Auburn hair like his father's, he was the spitting image of a young Owen while Edwina matched her mother in every way—including her feisty temperament.

"Because it's fun." The boy shrugged. Helen and Ben reminded him of Lily and he when they were younger, and he recognized a boyhood crush when he saw one.

"It's not polite to steal from your friends, Benjamin James!" Helen propped tiny fists on her hips and glared upward, not allowing the boy's sass to stand.

"She's right, dear. Come down and return whatever you've taken. Then both of you can join us for a picnic." Lily proffered the basket in her hand. Sufficiently enticed by the lure of food, Ben crawled down before handing over the red ribbon tied around his wrist.

"Here you go, Helen. You know I was just messing around."

The girl tipped her nose up haughtily as if she wouldn't forgive the lad, until she tapped the side of his arm yelling, "You're it!" and took off at a run.

"Does this mean they won't be joining us?" Lily asked, shaking her head at their antics.

"More for us." He winked, bending to kiss her cheek. Edwina climbed higher for a kiss, too, which he happily obliged. "Now, shall we dine? Wouldn't want my two favorite girls to starve."

Giggling, both of his loves agreed, and they found a shady spot under the recently vacated tree, animated chatter erupting amongst them.

He adored his life. Whatever hardships befell him in his youth, it was all worth it for this—a loving wife and two exuberant children.

He wouldn't have had it any other way.

THE END

THANK YOU FOR READING!

Please consider leaving a rating/review on Amazon and/or Goodreads. Ratings & reviews are the #1 way to support an indie author like me.

They don't have to be long or even positive (though I hope you enjoyed this book!). All the Amazon/Goodreads algorithms care about are QUANTITY.

The more reviews, the more Amazon/Goodreads show my books to other potential readers!

And they serve as guides to readers on whether or not to take a chance on an indie author.

To stay up-to-date on new releases and more, join my newsletter and follow me on Instagram: @authorjemmafrost!

I appreciate your support!

Happy Reading,

Jemma

ALSO BY JEMMA FROST

Charming Dr. Forrester
All Rogues Lead to Ruin
An Earl Like Any Other
The Scoundrel Seeks a Wife

ABOUT THE AUTHOR

Jemma Frost grew up in the Midwest where she visited the library every day and read romance novels voraciously! Now, she lives in North Carolina with her cat, Spencer, and dreams of stories to be written!

FOLLOW JEMMA FROST on Instagram and/or Facebook: @authorjemmafrost

Made in the USA
Monee, IL
07 November 2024